Wintering Well

Wintering Well

LEA WAIT

Margaret K. McElderry Books
New York   London   Toronto   Sydney

Margaret K. McElderry Books
An imprint of Simon & Schuster
Children's Publishing Division
1230 Avenue of the Americas
New York, New York 10020

Book design by Ann Sullivan
The text for this book is set in Centaur MT.
Manufactured in the United States of America
2 4 6 8 10 9 7 5 3 1

Library of Congress Cataloging-in-Publication Data
Wait, Lea.
Wintering well / Lea Wait.—1st ed.
p. cm.
Summary: Fifteen-year-old Will Ames and his sister Cassie go to stay
with their sister in nearby Wiscasset, Maine, after a disabling accident
ruins Will's plans for a career in farming.
ISBN 0-689-85646-6 (hardcover)
[1. Brothers and sisters—Fiction. 2. People with disabilities—
Fiction. 3. Family life—Maine—Fiction. 4. Maine—History—
19th century—Fiction.] I. Title.
PZ7.W1319Wi 2004
[Fic]—dc22
2003019322

For Abby and Ben Park, who showed me that a
disability may only be a curve in the road,
not a stop sign.

For Emma Dryden, who has enthusiasm, faith, insight, and
patience—what more could one ask of an editor?

And with thanks to Dr. Kathleen Reed,
who provided counsel.

CHAPTER I

THE JOURNAL OF CASSIE AMES

August 29, 1819, Woolwich, District of Maine

Today Ma gave me this journal. She said a girl of eleven should have a place to record private thoughts and dreams. She knows I have missed my sister, Alice, since she married Aaron Decker and moved to Wiscasset, and that I am not patient with household chores. Brothers are lively, but they are not people in whom to confide. All morning I thought of what I might write on these pages; what plans for my future I might record. But what happened this afternoon is too terrible to write. I pray for Will tonight, and I pray for mysef, because I am the cause of all that happened this day. Please, God, let Will live. And please, God, forgive me.

The fresh green smell of newly scythed summer wheat was too much to resist. Will took a deep breath, threw down his hay rake, and rolled over and over on the long, yellowed grasses, pushing his face deep into them, until one piece of hay stuck right into his nose and took him into a sneezing fit that stopped his rolling.

Laughing at himself, he got up, glanced around sheepishly to make sure no one had seen him, brushed himself off, and picked up the rake. Twelve was too old for such antics, there was no doubt, and his older brothers, Simon and Nathan, would be the first to call Pa's attention to such childish behavior. He brushed his sun-lightened hair away from his face and went back to work.

Simon and Nathan worked the farm because it was a fertile piece of land and someday they would each inherit a part of it. Ethan, at four, had his future far ahead of him. But Will had known he was destined to be a farmer since he was younger than Ethan. He remembered sitting in the dirt outside their farmhouse door, reaching down into the warm, moist soil, rubbing it over his hands, then tasting it in gulps before Ma caught him. The land was a part of him.

Will would be a farmer because it was his calling.

"It's in his blood," Pa would say as he smiled and answered Will's questions about why beans should be planted at the full moon, and why dried blood kept beetles away from the potato leaves. "Your brothers learn because they have to . . . you learn because your mind is on a quest for knowledge."

"Quest for knowledge or no," Ma would chime in,

"his clothes are dirtier than those of the other three boys combined. He'll never be able to farm this earth—he takes too much of it with him to his bed each night."

Will leaned on his rake and smiled at the memory. Reverend Adams said it was a gift to know your place in life. And he knew his. The grasses, the earth, the sky, the animals—they were all a part of him. They were his past and his present, and they would be his future.

His friend Jamie had also been born on a farm, but he hated the smell of manure and the uncertainty of crops. Jamie dreamed of being an apprentice in a shipyard. "To take a piece of wood and build a vessel that sails to the corners of the earth." That was Jamie's dream. Their friend Sam was promised as an apprentice to the silversmith and clock maker in Wiscasset.

They were all too old for school now, and Pa had said this winter Will's help would be needed with the clearing of more acres for spring planting. Lumbering had always been his older brothers' job. This would be the first season Will would be with them, farming like the other men. Will stood taller just thinking of it.

The late-August sun was hot, and the hay was set for drying. Will left the fields and headed back to the house. A cool drink, and then he would split more logs for the woodpile. Winter was the time for cutting trees and stacking them on sledges for the oxen to pull from the woods. Summer was the time to prepare wood for the fireplace. Trees felled last January were cut, split, and stacked now so the logs would be dry before the snows came. Each man in the household took his turn with the ax.

Will filled the tin cup hanging near the pump and drank deeply. Then he pumped another cup full and poured the cold water over his head to cool it down. His naturally pale skin was dark from field work, but he refused to wear a hat as his brothers did. Without a hat he could feel the heat from the sun radiate throughout his body, all the way to his toes, which were bare as often as possible. He hesitated a moment. No; his boots would have to stay on for wood splitting. He already imagined how good his toes would feel, released from the leather boots and splashed with cool well water. Soon enough.

He heard Simon and Pa calling to each other from the back pasture, where they were checking Susan, one of the cows, who had limped this morning at milking. Ma was singing over the rhythmic *thump-thump* of the butter churn. Cassie was no doubt playing with Sunshine, her new kitten, or racing through a field far from Ma's voice reminding her she was a young lady, not the fifth son in the family. Cassie would rather help a young bird back to its nest or watch the birth of a calf than knead bread or practice her stitches. Ethan would be with Ma.

Will pulled the ax out of the stump. Nathan had left it there before riding over to the Baileys' for a large wooden hammer to help repair the north pasture fence.

Nathan had found more and more excuses to stop at the Baileys' since sixteen-year-old Martha Bailey started smiling at him in church each Sunday. But he'd done his share of the splitting before he left. And he'd separated out a small pile of sugar maple scraps that might be good for carving. Will loved to find the creatures hidden inside wood and release them. He had filled a box with pine and maple animals for Ethan, and Ma displayed one of the crows he had carved on her kitchen windowsill. Birds were harder to shape than the moose and horses Ethan loved to play with.

Will glanced quickly at the maple chips. One was just right to become a small, plump chickadee. He'd never attempted a chickadee before. And—yes! There in the pile was a black feather, standing straight up, perhaps lost by a flying crow. Grandmother had always said a black feather found standing meant good luck. Perhaps the chickadee would be easier to carve than he anticipated.

He smiled as he picked a log from the pile and looked at it critically. It had been cut too long for their four-foot fireplace. He placed it between the two cross-shaped horses that had held thousands of logs for the Ames fireplace, and picked up the hickory-handled side ax. The task was so familiar he didn't have to think. With a blow to each side he scored the log, preparing it to be shortened.

He raised the ax for the final blow, when Cassie's scream broke his concentration.

"Help! No!"

Will spun around as Cassie ran down the hill from their small family burying ground. Her long brown hair and blue skirt were flying, her yellow kitten in her arms.

As Will turned, the ax in his hand fell. Its edge glanced off the side of the log and hit his left leg. The sharp, curved blade cut neatly through his high leather boot, through his skin, and into his bone. As Cassie reached him, thrusting Sunshine into his arms, the ax hit the ground, and they both looked down. Gushing blood had already soaked through his boot and was seeping onto the ground.

The five-foot black racer snake that had been chasing Cassie and Sunshine turned back toward the bushes.

"Ma!" Cassie screamed. "Ma! Pa! Help!"

A white slash of pain streaked through Will. He loosed his hold on Sunshine, who jumped to the ground and scrambled toward the house, leaving a trail of bloody paw prints in the dust.

CHAPTER 2

September 4

Will is still in great pain. Ma placed the ax that cut him blade-side up under his bed to stop the bleeding, as her mother and grandmother taught her, and now the bleeding is not so heavy as it was at first. She also put her largest kitchen knife under Will's pillow to cut his pain, but that does not seem to make a difference to his suffering. If only I had not allowed my fear of the snake to cause me to scream, then Will would be as always. I have confined Sunshine in the barn and I sit by Will's bed and do what I can to make him comfortable. No one has blamed me in words, but I know they think it was my foolishness that caused the accident. They are right. If I had been sweeping the kitchen floor as Ma had directed, then Will would not have been injured.

Will lay in silence on a trestle bed strung with rope to support its straw mattress in the small room next to the kitchen. In some houses this space was called the birth and death room, used when someone in the family needed to be close to others and to the heat of the fire. The Ames family had been blessed with good health; their small room was generally used for storage. Provisions for the coming winter were already stacked on shelves around the bedstead they had moved there.

Cassie sat next to Will on a small pine stool, periodically wiping his damp forehead with a cloth, and reading softly out loud from the Bible. It was stuffy. The small, windowless room was designed to keep warmth inside during winter. Ethan had put his favorite of all the black bears Will had carved for him on a shelf near Will's bed. "So Will won't be lonely," Ethan had said.

Every few minutes Cassie stopped reading. "Will, you must drink something." She tried to force a pewter spoon full of water between her brother's lips. He turned his head away, as the injured squirrel she had tried to help last springtime had done. The water dripped down his chin.

After the heavy bleeding had slowed, Ma had left Will's care to Cassie. Ma's help was needed with threshing and winnowing the wheat; potatoes must be harvested for winter. With one less worker tasks would take longer to complete. There was nothing to be done for Will but wait until his leg healed. Cassie had volunteered to sit with him, and her offer had been gratefully accepted.

Will's swollen foot, ankle, and lower leg were

wrapped tightly in many layers of linen. At first Ma had changed the linen every few hours, when blood soaked through the layers into the straw pallet on the bedstead. Now the bleeding had slowed, so the linen stayed in place longer. The bandages were stained dark red, but some of the blood was dry.

Will moaned. He slept most of the time, helped by Ma's crushed poppy seeds in brandy. Each year she put up a fresh bottle "against the time it be needed." Most summers she emptied the bottle onto the ground, untouched, before making more, but this year's bottle was already half empty. Cassie tried again to feed Will a spoonful of water. This time a few drops entered his mouth.

Suddenly his eyes opened. "Ma?" he asked. His voice was harsh and dry. "Ma?"

"Ma's out in the field. She's digging potatoes," said Cassie. "I'm here. Do you want more water? Or some bread?"

Will shook his head slightly. "My foot. The pain is like rain in a nor'easter, hitting again and again."

"The bleeding has slowed. You'll be well soon." Cassie felt Will's forehead. His skin was pale, but hot. "Try to eat something. Ma baked fresh anadama bread this morning. Your favorite."

He said nothing. His eyes were clouded.

"It's been six days; you haven't eaten a handful of food in all that time."

"Six days?" Will tried to focus on Cassie. "The wheat . . ."

"Pa and Nathan and Simon are bringing it in. Here, have a little more water."

Will opened his mouth and swallowed this time. His tongue looked white. He shivered despite the sweat on his forehead.

"I'm cold."

"I'll get you a quilt."

Cassie ran up the stairs to the chest in the sleeping chamber, where the quilts and blankets were stored in summer. She pulled out the red-and-blue one that Will had admired when Ma made it last March.

By the time she got back downstairs, Will had fallen asleep again. She tucked the quilt around him carefully. The weight on his foot made him moan, but she covered the rest of his body.

The room was hot, and Cassie felt dizzy. She picked up the Bible and started to read. "'The Lord is my shepherd . . .'"

CHAPTER 3

September 8

Will does not recognize us. His body is hot to the touch, and his leg is swelling, following the streaks of red that now rise above the dressing. Ma helped me remove the bandages today, which was not an easy task. Will cried out when they were pulled away from his skin. Under the coverings his wound is not healing well; what was red is now purple as dark lupine blossoms, and in some parts close to black. The smell is almost as unbearable to Ma and me as the pain is to Will. Pa refuses to enter the sickroom. He says we can do nothing; that Will's fate is in God's hands, not ours. I prayed and read from the Book of Job again today, but I do not know what Will could have done to require this testing. Perhaps it is me He is punishing, for not having thought before I acted. Perhaps I am not praying hard enough. I make what few amends are possible by keeping Will as comfortable as I can.

"The blackness in his leg means there is no hope. The boy is clearly going to die." Cassie, at Will's bedside as she had been all night, heard Pa's low voice from where he sat in the kitchen with Ma. "We have been lucky not to have lost any of our children before this."

Ma's voice rose. "Will is not dead! As long as he lives, we must not give up hope! We must not stop trying to save him!"

"You and Cassie have cared well for him. Give him as much of the poppy drink as he can take. It should help ease his pain."

"Send Simon or Nathan for Dr. Bradford, down to Bath. He helped John Palmer when the ox crushed his foot."

"His helping made John Palmer a cripple."

"Better a cripple than a dead man."

"What good is a man without a full body? What use to himself, or to anyone? Will's leg won't ever be normal. I've seen abscesses like that on animals. If he were a cow, like Susan, we'd be able to end his pain."

"You shot Susan."

"As was necessary. She was a cow, woman. Will is a boy. Why God allows a boy to suffer longer than a cow I do not attempt to know."

Ma's voice rose in shock. "You can't think of shooting Will as you did an animal!"

"I won't do it. But I can't say it hasn't crossed my

mind as he lies there, his moans reaching all of us. Even his smell is throughout the house."

Ma tried one more time. "Please. For my sake. Send one of the boys for the doctor. You're right; he may be able to do nothing. But my heart will better accept what has to come if we have tried everything possible to save him."

The legs of Pa's chair scraped on the pine floor as he pushed back from the table. "I need the boys in the field. If we don't get the crops in, we'll all starve next winter. There is no hope; the sooner you accept that, the better." Pa's voice softened. "Keep the boy comfortable, and trust it will be over soon, for all of our sakes."

Moments later Ma's crying was low and muffled. But Pa's hammer rang clear.

Cassie stood so abruptly she knocked over her stool. Will's body jerked at the sound. *No. It cannot be,* she thought. In the kitchen Ma was sobbing quietly, her apron pulled almost over her head. Ethan had left the carved horses he had been playing with and was patting her leg. Cassie talked quickly. "Ma, yesterday I saw Pa pulling out those planked logs he was saving to build a buttery. But that's not what he's doing, is it? Pa's making Will's coffin, isn't he?"

Ma nodded into her apron.

Cassie put her arm around Ma. Her voice didn't waver. "I know what you'll say, but you cannot stop me. It was my doing that put Will in this state. I have to help."

Ma looked up, her face red and swollen with weeping. "What more can you do than care for him as you are doing?"

"I can go for a doctor. I can ride near as well as the boys, and I'm no use in the field. We won't starve for my absence."

"Cassie, no. You should not have been listening. Your father is right. We have to accept what God wills."

"If Will should die, then we'll have no choice. But he is not yet dead, and I am going." She quickly untied her apron and handed it to Ma. "I'll return as soon as I can. I know I must honor you and Pa. But I have to do this. Please understand."

Ma did not try to stop her.

CHAPTER 4

Cautiously Cassie headed Sarah, their old mare, down the narrow road, deeply scarred by the tracks wagon wheels had made in spring mud. The deep ruts made it unsafe to go very fast. After a mile the road would divide and, at that point, would widen. Then they would be able to go more quickly. But in which direction?

Cassie talked quietly to the horse. "If we turn right, that will mean six miles of riding south to the ferry that crosses the Kennebec River to Bath, where Dr. Bradford is. That's the shortest way. But I don't know if the ferry is running today, or if someone would give us free passage. And Pa did not speak highly of Dr. Bradford." She patted the horse gently and kept talking. "Maybe Pa would better accept another doctor. If we turn left, we'll go north, toward Wiscasset, where Alice is. The road is a little longer, but there are no rivers to cross. And Alice will help us. There must be a doctor in Wiscasset."

Without hesitating, Cassie turned north at the fork.

Even here, where the hard earth road was wider, there were rocks and branches in the path. Sarah picked her way between them. Cassie failed to notice a low branch, which scraped her face. It would take longer to reach Wiscasset than she had imagined. But she could not hurry; if Sarah were injured, then she, like Susan the cow, would be unfit for work. The mare might be old, but her strength was essential to the farm. She pulled their wagon to church on Sundays; she carried them to nearby farms for supplies or friendship. Without her the Ames family would be much more isolated.

Cassie patted Sarah. She tried not to think of how much pain Will was in, or what the time was, or what Pa would say when he discovered she had gone.

It was late morning before she drew up in front of Alice's small whitewashed house on Middle Street, just two blocks from John Stacy's store, where Alice's husband, Aaron, worked. Quickly she tied Sarah to the granite horse block and ran to the door.

"Cassie! What has happened? Why are you here?" Alice held her sister at arm's length. Cassie's long hair was matted, and her dark blue dress was soaked with sweat. "No matter the cause—you're in need of a long drink, and something to eat if you've ridden all the way from home."

Cassie nodded as she tried to speak, and gestured toward her horse.

"And of course Sarah, too, should have water. Aaron!" Alice turned toward the back of the house, "Aaron, come quickly! Cassie's here."

Alice's stocky young husband came out from the back room, still holding the pewter tankard he had been drinking from. "What has happened that your ma and pa sent you all this way alone?"

Cassie shook her head again.

"I'll get her something to drink and a place to sit. You care for her horse." Alice guided Cassie toward the kitchen.

A few minutes later, after managing to swallow a small glass of water, Cassie was able to talk.

"Pa did not send me. I left. Will is hurt. Bad. His ax slipped." Cassie took a deep breath. "It was all my fault, Alice. I screamed because I saw a black snake, and it startled him. His left leg is swollen and blackening, and Pa says he is dying, but Ma wanted a doctor, and so I took Sarah and came. He needs a doctor. Quick!"

"Poor Will!" Alice hesitated only a moment. "Dr. Theobold lives close by. Aaron will go and tell him how to get to the farm. You sit and rest."

"I have to go back." Cassie started to get up. "I want to be with Will. And Ma and Pa will be worried about me."

Alice looked at her little sister again. "You're too weary to ride back now, and Sarah needs rest. We'll ask Dr. Theobold to take both of us back in his wagon.

Aaron can bring Sarah in a few days and fetch me home. I should be with the family too."

Cassie squeezed her sister's hand.

"I knew it was right to come to you, Alice. The doctor will help. He'll make Will well!"

"I hope so, Cassie. I hope so."

CHAPTER 5

September 8, late afternoon
In the confusion Pa has not even scolded me for leaving
without permission, and after a moment's hesitation he
hugged me in silent thanks when he saw Alice and the
doctor. Now is not the moment to talk with him. Dr.
Theobold has examined Will's leg, but his expression is
not hopeful as he talks with Pa and Ma in the kitchen
yard. Alice is preparing supper, and I should be help-
ing, but I cannot until I know whether my fetching of a
doctor has helped. Perhaps there is no use. But I could
not give Will up without knowing he had every possible
chance. I pray Dr. Theobold can save him. He must.

Dr. Theobold's voice was low as he spoke with Ma and
Pa. "The boy will die, and soon, if the leg is not
removed. And there is only a chance that surgery can
keep him alive. He has been weakened by the gangrene.
More than half of such patients die."

Pa shook his head. "So you will cause him more pain, and he may die anyway? And if he should live . . . his life has already been lost. How can a man farm without a leg?"

"But he might live! If he does, we will have time to help him learn to live without a leg. If the doctor does not try, there will be no time." Ma looked pleadingly at her husband. "Remember how Will loves the sunlight and the smells of the barn and field? Let the doctor do what he can. Give Will this chance."

Pa hesitated. Nathan and Simon stood near the kitchen door, keeping Ethan away and hoping to overhear the decision. "We have three fine sons left," he finally said. "Will is going to be a burden to the family for the rest of his life if he lives a cripple."

"Mr. Ames, there are professions not requiring a leg. Many fine soldiers in the War of 1812 lost limbs and walk with crutches or with wooden legs." Dr. Theobold hesitated. "But it won't be easy for Will, it is true. Or for any of you. And I would need assistance with the surgery itself."

Ma looked up at him. "Whatever you need, we will provide."

Pa looked from her to the doctor. "My wife is right, Doctor. We'll do what we can to help you."

Dr. Theobold touched both of their arms. "You're doing what is best for the boy. This is his only chance." He saw Nathan and Simon in the doorway. "I'll need

two strong men to help hold Will while I'm working."
He looked again at Pa. "It won't be easy to watch."

Pa nodded. "Nathan and I will do what needs to be
done."

"Good. Mrs. Ames, have you sand to scour your
floor?"

"In the back shed."

"You must get it. We'll use your kitchen table for the
surgery; the light is better there than in the room where
Will is now. Put the table near the window, leaving
room to walk around it, and layer the floor with all the
sand you have."

Ma looked at him questioningly.

"The sand is to help absorb the blood, so none of
us will slip. Put an old blanket on the table to help cush-
ion Will. Bring me clean linens that I may use as dressings. And make sure the fire is high."

Ma walked quickly toward the house.

Dr. Theobold looked again at Pa. "The younger
children should not be in the room. But if your wife
could stay to help with the fire and to fetch anything I
might have need of, that would be helpful. Can she do
that?"

Mr. Ames looked after his wife. "If she must."

"I will get my instruments from the wagon. You talk
with your family. And gather any liquor you have in the
house."

It did not take long for the preparations to be made.

Nathan agreed to help, as did Ma. Simon and Alice took Ethan outside.

"Please, sir, I would like to help," said Cassie to Dr. Theobold. "I have been tending Will. I know what his leg is like."

The doctor looked at Ma. She hesitated and then nodded.

"If any of you feel faint, move outside. Do not feel ashamed. It happens. But I cannot have anyone fainting and knocking against Will or me while I am operating."

Cassie shook her head. "I will not faint."

Dr. Theobold pulled needles, pins, forceps, knives, and two saws, one larger than the other, from his box and laid them on a counter near the table. "I will need hot water, a kettleful," he directed. "Heat this in the fire," he added, handing Ma a three-inch-wide strip of iron with a wooden handle. "And be sure this is hot." He handed her a tin pail of hardened tar.

Pa and Nathan picked Will up and carried him to the table. Thankfully, Will did not seem to know what was happening. "Give him as much rum as he can take," the doctor directed Cassie. "The liquor may help dull his pain."

Cassie took the bottle from Pa and started spooning the rum down Will's throat. He choked, and looked about in confusion, but swallowed. Dr. Theobold removed the dressings from Will's leg. Pa and Nathan both stepped back; they had not seen the swollen and blackened limb

Ma and Cassie had been tending. The dense odor of decaying flesh filled the room.

"Mr. Ames, I need you to hold Will up so his legs are over the side of the table." The doctor showed Pa how to stand, his arms under Will's shoulders and his hands clasped across Will's chest. "Nathan, kneel on the floor and hold Will's bad leg up so it is level from the thigh to the knee."

Will's leg had swollen to twice its usual size. But after a moment's hesitation Nathan knelt in the sand on the floor and did as directed.

"Mrs. Ames, keep the linens available, and bring what is needed as I tell you."

Ma's face was as pale as thin milk.

"Cassie, you said you have been caring for Will."

"Yes, sir."

"Can you stand the sight of blood?"

Cassie's answer was steady. "Yes. I can."

"Good. Then, take this sponge." He handed her a dry, red-tinged sea sponge from his medical box. "When I say so, clean Will's wound and soak up as much blood as you can, squeeze it out on the sand quickly, and then return the sponge for more. I need to see the wound clearly as I cut and stitch."

Cassie focused her eyes on the sponge and on her brother's leg. "I can do that."

Dr. Theobold picked up a large knife. "May God bless us and bless Will this day. May we have the skill and strength to do what we can to help this boy, and may God give him the strength to survive and to live in His service. Amen."

It all happened as quickly as possible. Dr. Theobold cut the flesh around the thigh bone, and then as Pa struggled to hold Will's jerking body Ma handed the doctor the larger saw, and he cut the bone. The sharp grating sound of the saw cutting the bone filled the kitchen. As two thirds of Will's leg fell onto the kitchen floor, Nathan vomited. But he did not get in the doctor's way.

Cassie could not look at the leg on the floor. She concentrated on mopping up the blood as the doctor had directed, while he pulled the flesh down over the exposed thighbone, cauterized it with the hot poker, and stitched the flesh together. He then painted the hot tar over the wound and, after it had cooled and dried, covered it with the clean dressings.

Will had not moved since after the first knife finished.

Pa and Dr. Theobold carried him back into the chamber that had become his, and the doctor showed Cassie and Ma how to pull another dressing over the stump of his leg and pin this outside dressing to the bedding. "What is left of the leg will shake, and perhaps jerk, with the pain. The binding is to help keep the boy steady on the bed."

While Cassie and Ma arranged the bedding, Pa removed the severed leg and Alice silently scrubbed the kitchen floor. Despite the sand, which was now soaked with blood and vomit, blood had stained the wide pine boards too deeply to be erased.

As Will slept restlessly, the doctor joined the family for the supper of beef stew Alice had made earlier.

At first nothing was said. Even little Ethan was silent. Finally Cassie asked, "Was your surgery a success, Doctor?"

"The surgery was successful, Cassie. He has a good chance to live. But he needs much care. I will leave you a solution made from the young branches of the white willow tree. My father was a doctor in Germany before he came to this country, and he brought seedlings of the tree with him. Try to give Will a spoonful every hour. The solution should help his fever break. Do you have any pussy willows nearby?"

Surprised, Nathan answered, "Some grow on the edge of the woods in back of the east pasture."

"Good. Tomorrow cut some of the branches, remove the bark, and put it in water, and then boil the solution down some. Use it to bathe Will's stump once a day. It should help reduce the inflammation. Keep him quiet. Make sure he drinks and eats what he can." Dr. Theobold hesitated. "Many patients feel pain from a limb that is gone. Do not think the boy is crazed if he complains his severed leg still gives him pain. The pain will end in time."

In the next room Will moaned. He was the only one who did not know this day had changed his life.

CHAPTER 6

September 10

Alice has returned to Wiscasset, and I am back by Will's bedside. He sleeps fitfully, but the willow tea helps; his body is not as hot as it was. Ma assists me in changing the dressing, but Will's care appears to be mine. I cannot concentrate on mending Ethan's shirt, which I should be doing. I look at Will and at the space where his leg used to be. I wonder whether his mind has changed, as his body has. I wonder if he will spend the rest of his life on this pallet. I wonder if I will have to spend the rest of mine sitting next to him. I wonder if he really shall live, as Dr. Theobold hoped.

Will opened his eyes. Cassie was next to him, stitching a garment of some sort. He blinked. His throat was parched.

"Water."

Cassie started. "Will! You're awake!" In a moment

she was back with a porringer of water and a pewter spoon.

Will started to sit up but then dropped back and let Cassie spoon the cool water between his dry lips. He swallowed several spoonfuls. The room was dim. "Is it day?"

"It is midday. Friday."

"I've been sleeping."

"You have been feverish." Cassie hesitated. "Alice came, with a doctor from Wiscasset. You are better now."

"I've been no use to Pa. I must get up."

"Not yet, Will. You need to rest more. You need to heal."

"My leg still hurts. Every time I move my toes, my whole body hurts."

Cassie didn't reply.

Will lay quietly for a while. Then, suddenly, he started to sit up. "Cassie, I need to go to the privy."

Cassie turned. "You are not strong enough to get to the privy. I have a chamber pot." She reached over to the covered pot she had kept in the corner of the room for her own use so she would not have to leave him.

"I don't need that." Suddenly Will looked at the lines of his body under the blankets. "Cassie. My leg. It's . . ." He shook his head in disbelief. "I can't see my leg."

"Your leg was swollen and blackened. It would have killed you." She looked into Will's blue eyes and said it out straight. "The doctor had to cut it off. So you would live."

Cassie stood holding the chamber pot. Will looked down again at his body.

"NO!!!!!" His scream filled the room, echoing all the pain of the past days. "NO!!!" He tried again to get up. Cassie moved to help him, but his arm struck out, knocking the chamber pot from her hands. As it hit the floor, it shattered, its contents and pieces of china flying. "NO!"

Cassie stood silently. Her eyes filled with tears.

Will collapsed back. "Why couldn't I have just died?"

Sunshine appeared at the doorway. She walked delicately to the mess on the floor and sniffed, then jumped up on the bed, turning herself around and settling where Will's leg should have been.

Will turned his face toward the wall and sobbed.

CHAPTER 7

October 17

Dr. Theobold came again. He says Will's leg is healing well and soon he should be strong enough to use a crutch. The stump of his leg is still swollen, but less so. The doctor showed me how to tighten the dressings so the bleeding doesn't start again. Will helps now with the dressing, although I believe I am still more used to see-ing his leg—or what used to be his leg—than he is. He sleeps long hours. There is little for him to do. I read aloud when he wishes it and do my chores in his room when I can to keep him company. Some days I feel I am as much a prisoner in this room as is Will. Mattie and Tempe stopped to visit for a few minutes on their way home from the schoolhouse yesterday. I do not miss les-sons, but I do miss their company. They were full of news about an apple bee to be held at Tempe's home next Saturday to celebrate the harvest and prepare apples for drying. Martha Bailey is sure to hope her apple peel takes the shape of an N when she throws it over her shoulder, since clearly she has set her hopes on marrying Nathan. Ma and Pa plan on going to the bee, as well as Nathan and Simon. I will stay with Will and Ethan. I have promised to stay with Will so long as he needs me, and Ethan is no trouble. Perhaps it is my fate to be without company, as Will's fate is to be a cripple. He says little. Each day I wake hoping he will smile. As yet he has not. Some days I do not either.

"Will, wake up and get yourself together. You have guests!" Ma walked in briskly, bringing with her the smell of autumn leaves and the apple cider she had been making the day before. Will turned over, and Ma handed him a clean shirt. "Put this on. Your friends Jamie and Sam were at services and have come to visit you."

It was a beautiful October Sunday, the air sharp with the beginning of winter, the yellow and orange leaves of the sugar maples covering the fading grasses.

The Ames family, all but Will, had spent the morning in church. Even Cassie had gone this week.

Will rubbed his eyes and struggled to pull himself up on the pallet and pull on the shirt. He and Jamie and Sam had been friends since they were babies learning to walk at church picnics. They'd explored the woods together, handed notes to one another under their school desks, and spent hours fishing and talking of their futures. No one could have closer friends. For the first time since his accident he grinned as they walked into the small room.

They stood near the door, awkwardly shifting from one foot to another. Jamie spoke first. "Hello, Will. We've missed you." He did not look at the place Will's leg should have been. "How are you?"

Sam laughed slightly and turned red with embarrassment. "We know what happened. We are sorry, Will."

They looked at each other self-consciously. "We should have come before this," added Jamie. "But it is a busy time. Harvest chores. You know."

"Get another stool from the kitchen so you both can sit down," Will answered. From where he lay he had to look up to see them. It would be easier if they were all on one level. "It is so good to see you! Tell me all the news."

They relaxed a little as Sam pulled up the other stool.

"This week I leave for Bath. I am to work at Stetson's Shipyard," Jamie shared proudly. "You know how many years I have dreamed of this! I will be cleaning up and fetching things and watching at first, but soon I hope to be a full apprentice. By the time I am eighteen, I should be well on my way to being a master shipwright. And I will be close enough to home to come back for holidays and such."

"That's wonderful news, Jamie," Will said quietly.

"I am leaving too," added Sam. "I stayed as long as I could, but now that Jamie is going, and you . . ." He hesitated, then rushed on, "And there is no reason to stay longer; I'm going over to Wiscasset to work for Mr. Sullivan Wright, to learn silversmithing and clock making. I will be living near your sister Alice. Maybe in a few years I will be making a clock for her and her husband!"

Will brushed a tear away, hoping no one had seen. Jamie and Sam were going on with their lives. He was staying.

Finally Sam broke the silence. "Are you . . . going to be all right, Will?"

Will spoke a bit louder than necessary. "Dr. Theobold, from over to Wiscasset, says I am healing and should be just fine soon. Pa is going to make a crutch for me so I can start walking again."

"When we are home for Thanksgiving, we can all get together," Sam said.

Will thought of what they always did together. Tobogganing, skating on Abner's Pond, snowshoeing through the woods.

Jamie and Sam must have thought the same thing. "We will come and see you then. When we are home again," said Jamie.

"I will write to you from Wiscasset," Sam added.

"I would like that."

There was another long silence. Finally Jamie cleared his throat. "We should be starting to home. We don't want to tire you."

Will nodded. He was not tired, but there was nothing more to say. He could not remember a time when there was nothing to say to Jamie and Sam. They were moving on to other lives. He was trapped in a windowless room, unable even to go to the privy by himself.

CHAPTER 8

November 13

I am writing by light of a candle when I should be to bed. Today I was not patient with Will, and now I cannot sleep because of it. There is so much to be done to prepare for Thanksgiving dinner, and he does nothing to help. I am weary trying to meet his needs and those of Ma and the rest of the family. Some days I am proud to be doing what is necessary, the same as a grown woman must. But I do miss seeing Mattie and Tempe and the other girls. To be sure, I see much of Will and Ma and Ethan, who is sweet but everywhere he should not be, and I see the older boys and Pa at supper time, but still I feel very alone. There is no one to talk with about plans for the holiday, or any of the other thoughts that fill my head. Ma is too busy; Alice is too far away; and the boys would not understand. Sometimes, as today, I do not behave as I should. I must learn patience. Ma says it is my age, as if the

*number of years a person has been alive changes her
mood. But it is not being eleven years old that is hard.
It is being in this house for days at a time and watching Will do nothing but stare at the wall. If only life
could be as it was before I screamed at seeing that silly
snake. I wonder if Ma or Alice ever felt as though the
walls of a house were like those of a prison.*

"Cassie, get me some more apple pie. I have finished
mine." Will sat in the chair he favored, near the kitchen
window. Again today he had not dressed below his
waist, but covered both his stump and his good leg with
a quilt. The wooden crutch Pa had made leaned against
the wall next to him.

"The rest of the pie is just on the table; you can get
it." Cassie was kneading a large bowl of dough for the
day's bread, and her hands were covered with flour. Ma
had left early this morning for young Mrs. Evans' home.
Mrs. Evans was near her time, and Ma had promised to
be there to help her prepare for the new baby. She had
left the Ames kitchen to Cassie.

"I can wait until you have time." Will looked out at
the small patch of the yard. Some days he looked out
that window for hours.

"Cassie, may I have some pie too?" Ethan crawled
out from under the kitchen table and pulled Cassie's
apron strings.

She grabbed at him and at the apron. "Ethan, I'm

busy! Leave my apron alone. And you have already had two pieces of pie. You do not need another now."

"Will is going to have another."

"Will is not going to have another unless he gets up out of his chair and gets it himself."

"But Cassie, Will's leg is hurt."

"He could walk better if he'd practice more with the crutch. His leg is healing."

"This morning it really aches, Cassie. You cannot know what the pain is like. You don't know what my life is like. And even if I did get myself to the table, what would be the use?"

"The use would be you could get your own apple pie. And if you want to be of help, there is plenty you could do. There is pumpkin to be cleaned and sliced before it's strung in the attic to dry. There's pewter to be scoured before Thanksgiving. There are pieces of pork and suet and herbs to be chopped for mincemeat, if you want a pie. Or you could read a story to Ethan or play a game with him to keep him away from my apron strings!" Cassie retied her apron with her floury fingers. "There is plenty to do. All you do is sit and carve those stupid animals for Ethan."

Will concentrated on the moose he was carving. Its antlers were not right yet. "All that is women's work. Not work for a man."

"Well, if you cannot do a man's work, then you had better find something else to do!"

Will's face reddened and his hands clenched around

the moose so hard one of its legs broke off. He threw the broken animal, hard, against the wall.

Cassie stopped kneading, wiped her hands on her apron, and went over to Will. "Forgive me. That was cruel. It is just that I am tired, and I really could use your help. Please."

Will scowled at her. "I will cut up the pumpkins, if I must, if you bring them to me. But I will not do any cooking!"

"Fine!" Cassie pulled a large basket full of small sugar pumpkins from the corner and set it next to him. "You have no trouble eating, I notice."

Ethan picked up the broken moose from the floor. "Will, the moose has a broken leg. Can you carve a crutch for him so he can walk again?"

A knock on the door stopped further talking. It was Reverend Adams.

"I was in the neighborhood and thought I would pay a short call on Will." The reverend walked in, speaking to Cassie. "I hope the time is not inconvenient."

"You are always welcome, of course, Reverend Adams," she answered, pulling over a chair for him. "I'm sorry, but Ma is to the Evans place this morning, and Pa and the boys went over to Bath for supplies."

Will winced. Three months ago he had been one of "the boys."

"I am sorry to have missed them, but it is Will I have come to see."

"It would be well if he had someone new to talk with, I'm sure." Cassie gestured at Will. "Would you care for some molasses cakes and cider?"

"Can I have cakes too?" Ethan smiled in delight at having company. "Cakes are very good."

"If your sister says you may," answered the reverend. "But I would like to visit with your brother for a short time."

Will looked at him. "I am here."

"So you are. We have missed you in church these past weeks." Reverend Adams pulled his chair closer to Will's so they could talk quietly.

Will looked at him incredulously. "I cannot walk. I have only one leg."

"True. But you have a crutch, I see. And I am sure your pa and brothers would carry you if you could not walk the distance from the wagon to the church."

"I am not a baby! I do not wish to be carried!"

"Well, then, since you have missed services, perhaps we could pray a bit here this morning." Cassie moved a stool next to Reverend Adams and put a plate of molasses cakes and some cider on it. Ethan reached over and took two cakes, one for each hand. Cassie headed him back to the far end of the kitchen.

"I have prayed," said Will, "and it is of no use. God let me be crippled. He has not healed me. He has not answered my prayers."

"No doubt your accident was God's will. All that

happens in the world is God's will. But He has answered your prayers. You are alive!"

"I do not live. I breathe, I eat. But how can God leave me like this? My life was planned! You know—I was going to be a farmer. How can I do that now?"

"Perhaps God has another plan for you. In God's eyes all things are made to meet a purpose. Why else would He have made apples round to fit easily in a hand?"

"Well, He has not told me what His plan is for me. I should have died. I would rather have died if I cannot sow and harvest crops, and milk the cow, and lumber the woods. How can I be anything but a cripple in a kitchen chair now? God took away my life."

"He left you your life, Will. He took away your leg."

"He took away my dreams."

"Then, you must find new ones. With His help."

Will sat, silent.

That night the family woke out of a deep sleep to hear a crash and a cry. Cassie reached the top of the stairs just as Pa did. "Will!"

By the time they got down to Will's room and lit a candle, he had pulled himself up to a sitting position on the floor.

"What happened, son?" Pa reached over to help Will back onto his bed. Sunshine, who had chosen to leave Cassie's bed in favor of Will's, streaked around the corner.

"I was sleeping, and I thought I heard Ethan calling. He had fallen into the fireplace. He was calling me. I had to go to him; I had to get him out of the fire." Will hesitated. "I did not remember I could not walk." He turned his head away from Cassie and Pa and sobbed.

CHAPTER 9

Thanksgiving, November 25

I am almost too tired to write, since this day I have worked and eaten and talked enough for three. The family is together again. Alice and Aaron joined us for the holiday, and Will's friend Sam also stopped in. Ma and Alice and I were up before the sun this morning to put pies and bread to bake, and to prepare the turkey Nathan shot and the ham we smoked in September. All of us—even Will, leaning on his crutch and Pa's shoulder—went to church. After church we ate, and then Ma and Alice and I did the cleaning up, leaving the men to talk. We women did our share of talking too and found much to discuss. It is good to have Alice with us.

"The hope that Maine will become an independent state has been common talk in the taverns and streets of Wiscasset since two thirds of the District of Maine citizens voted in July to separate us from Massachusetts." Aaron raised his tumbler to the other men.

"Here on the farm we've had other concerns this season. We are interested, but no one here has the time to sit at a tavern table and debate issues of the world." Pa leaned toward Aaron. "Do you think it's going to happen this time? Maine will be a state?"

"Difficult to say for sure. On the first Monday in December there will be town meetings all over Maine, where we can vote on whether or not to accept the state constitution our delegates wrote down to Portland. The agreement we have with Massachusetts says we will separate from her if Congress accepts us as a state by next March fourth. We cannot apply to Congress to be a state until the constitution is voted on. And southern states that support slavery do not want Maine coming in as a free state. They say it would upset the balance; give the north a majority of votes. So we cannot assume Congress will vote us into the Union."

Pa smiled. "Makes Maine sound pretty important to have the whole Congress debating her." He turned to Will's friend. "Do you hear all that in Wiscasset too, Sam?"

"Yes, sir." Sam sat a little straighter, proud to be included in the circle of men. "And there is much talk about whether 'Maine' is the right name for us, and whether farming or sailing should be pictured on our state seal."

"Well, that is easy to decide," Nathan put in. "Got to be farming. You cannot bake bread out of fish! Without farmers, where would be the food for our Thanksgiving dinners?"

"But those spices in the pumpkin pie and mince-meat tasted pretty fine, and they came from trade with the Indies," Simon said.

"Why do folks feel it is finally time for the District of Maine to go off on its own?" Pa asked Aaron.

"If we were separated from Massachusetts, those gentlemen down in Boston wouldn't be able to give our tax money to their Harvard and Williams Colleges and allocate practically nothing to our Bowdoin. We'd have our own judges. And if another war should come, we'd defend ourselves, and not let the British invade our state, as Massachusetts let them invade Castine during the War of 1812. Our own governor would understand what was important to us. We wouldn't just be 'that wilderness district down east.'" Aaron's voice rose as he got more excited.

"Well, don't get yourself all churned up, Aaron. There is always something to talk about." Pa stretched out his legs and patted his stomach. "Would be nice to get to town more often, to keep up with the news, though. And it would be a grand thing if we were to be our own state and could make our own rules and decide where our tax money is to be spent. Be sure to write and let us know how it is all coming."

"For certain, I will."

"Last time we heard news was when your Dr. Theobold stopped in to see Will." Pa looked at Will. "The doctor says he's doing fine. Walking a little with his crutch. But what the boy is to do but help his Ma in the kitchen, I couldn't say. Not much use for a cripple on a farm."

Will shrank. Pa talked as though he weren't there.

Sam spoke up. "In Wiscasset a man about Simon's age, name of Jeremiah Crocker, has a hand crippled from an accident on the wharves. But he works at the county offices. And I have seen Mr. Peleg Tallman. He's an old man now, but he lost his left arm in a sea battle during the Revolution, and he is on the board of the Lincoln and Kennebec Bank and owns a shipyard over to Bath."

"That is true about Tallman, sure enough. He has two big houses, too. One on the other side of Woolwich and another in Bath. But he is a schooled man and had high friends in Boston to help him out in the beginning." Pa shook his head. "He is a very different person from our Will."

"Maybe Will could get a wooden leg." Sam looked sideways at his friend.

"I am no wooden doll," Will sputtered. "What could I do with a stick of wood where my leg should be? You don't know what you are speaking of."

Aaron looked at him. "I had not planned to say

anything just now, but Sam may have a thought. I was talking to Dr. Theobold last week, and he mentioned it, knowing Will is my brother-in-law."

"Mentioned what?" Pa put down his tankard.

"The possibility of Will's getting a new leg. Would not be easy, the doctor said, but if Will would work at getting used to one, then it could be done. Dr. Theobold said with a new leg Will could walk pretty well, and both of his hands would be free from the crutch."

"If I would work . . . what did he mean?" Will asked.

"First you would have to be completely healed. At least six months, he said, after the accident. And then a carpenter or cabinetmaker would make the leg. There would have to be a harness and padding to hold it on. And as you grow you would have to have new legs made."

"You could walk again, without help!" Sam grinned at Will.

"No running races, you understand," Aaron cautioned. "And you would have to be close to the doctor while you were getting used to the whole rig. Could be painful for a time."

"I am not afraid of pain." Will was defiant. "I have pain without a new leg. But even with a wooden leg, how could I plow damp earth or climb stairs or work in the barn loft?"

"True. Those things would be hard. But at least you could get to the privy yourself, even in the snow!" Simon said.

Will turned scarlet. How could Simon mention such things with everyone here? Not being able to manage the crutch on rough ground for long enough to get himself even to the privy was the worst part of not having a leg. Cassie or Simon helped him sometimes, but most times he still used the chamber pot inside, and Cassie emptied it. He hated that chamber pot. Most of all he hated depending on Cassie or Simon.

Pa's voice broke the awkward silence. "Sounds as though it would take some trouble to get such a leg, especially since we live far from those folks in Wiscasset who could make it happen. And even with the leg, Will is right that he still could not farm, or do much of anything, as far as I can see. Will is a cripple, and that is his burden, and ours. We can manage just fine the way things are." Pa stood up. "It is getting late. Sam, you need to get on the road before the dark is any thicker."

Our burden? Will held in his anger. How could Pa know what it felt like to have everyone ignoring him? Making decisions for him? Will's fingernails cut into the palms of his hands. His leg was gone, true. But Pa was acting as though Will's brain had been cut off too. He watched Pa wishing Sam a safe journey, just as though Sam were a grown man.

Sam nodded at Pa and put on his jacket. "It was good to see you, Will. And I promise to write. With the snows coming on, I probably will not be visiting again until spring."

Will looked at his friend, who was going back to a life far from the kitchen. "Winter well, Sam."

"And you. I will see you in spring, when the snows and mud are gone."

CHAPTER 10

March 7, 1820—STATE OF MAINE
Mr. Evans was just here to share the news. Last Friday President Monroe signed the bill making Maine the twenty-third state! The official birthday of the STATE OF MAINE will be March 15, but I am so excited I have to write it down now! Two new states will be added to the Union on the same day: Maine and Missouri. Maine will be added as a free state, and Missouri as a slave state. We will have our own governor and our own men representing us in Washington. Pa says now we can elect our own governor and make our own decisions on schools and local laws and taxes. He and the boys went with Mr. Evans to share the good news with other families and, I suspect, to celebrate at each home with a bit of rum. Ma and I and Will and Ethan had some cider and cakes to celebrate. We citizens of Maine have been recognized as independent from citified folks down in Massachusetts.
HURRAH FOR THE STATE OF MAINE!!

That winter was bleaker than Will could have imagined. Instead of going to school with Jamie and Sam, or lumbering with Pa and his brothers, he was confined to the three rooms on the first floor of their house. He padded the top of his crutch, so he no longer had sores under his arm, and he paced up and down the kitchen for hours each day. When he could walk no longer, he carved. Squirrels, skunks, cows, woodchucks—every windowsill in the house was now covered with small animals, and he had started working on an entire Noah's ark for Ethan. Today, as many days, he was restless.

"Will, you'll wear a trench in the floor if you keep up that pacing," Ma said as she stood at the table kneading the day's bread. Cassie had taken down some of the bacon smoked in the chimney and made a pie with apples dried in October. The kitchen smelled warm and sweet, but it was dark, although the hour was still early. Snowdrifts had long since covered the first-floor windows and kept out the sun. "Why don't you sit and read?"

"I have read the Bible through twice and almost memorized *McGuffey's Reader*," Will answered. "There is nothing else to read."

Ma sighed. "Well, read the Bible again. Might do you some good. Or carve another animal for Ethan."

Cassie sat rocking in a corner, knitting a yellow shawl to wear on Easter Sunday. "How does that special sock I knit you feel, Will?"

"It fits well, Cassie. You did a fine job." Cassie had knit Will a warm cover for his stump, as she had noticed it was especially sensitive to the cold. And this winter had been twice as cold as zero.

"Shall I knit another?"

Will thought a minute. "Perhaps a lighter one. For spring. This cold can't hang on much longer. Pa says he will start tapping the maple trees and sugaring off next week, and that's a sure sign of spring. We'll be on the downhill side of March in no time."

"March is often the month for the biggest storms," Ma pointed out. "But that sweet maple syrup will taste fine on some clean snow, for sure."

"I will eat a whole bucket of maple syrup snow," declared Ethan, who had carefully placed his wooden animals on the floor in the shape of an E, for Ethan, as Cassie had taught him. "I will put syrup on all the snowballs in my fort."

"Better choose some cleaner snow for the syrup. Those snowballs of yours have been frozen since December," Cassie said. "But having maple syrup to pour on pancakes and puddings again will be something special. We haven't had any since last November."

"All winter I have been trapped here. And soon it will be mud season." Will sat down suddenly. The thought of negotiating the deep Maine mud that came as sure as April after the snow and ice melted was a daunting one. "I have been thinking about what Dr. Theobold said. About a wooden leg. Ma, do you think we could find a way for me to try one? I cannot spend the rest of my life in this kitchen. Maybe with the leg I could do something. Perhaps not farming. Pa says I would be no use at that, and he may be right. But there must be something I can do."

"Are you certain that is truly what you want, Will?" Ma spoke gently. "A wooden leg might not work well. It might be another disappointment."

"Sam writes from Wiscasset about men who are printers, teachers, shopkeepers, barbers, blacksmiths, sailmakers . . . there must be a job there for me. My one leg is fine. It has strengthened as I have walked with the crutch. My arms are strong, and I still have a mind."

Ma looked at him. "But you need assistance. Cassie helps you to dress, and we are all here when you need to reach things. Your walking with the crutch is fine and steady in the house, but we do not know how far you could walk without exhausting yourself. You are not ready to be on your own yet."

Cassie put her knitting aside for a moment. Will's strength was back; that was certain. But how could he manage without her?

"But I must be able to take care of myself, Ma! Don't you see? If I stay here too long, then I will never leave. If I don't go, I'll be like Blind Annie, over to Bath, who has not left her home in forty years."

"I'll think on it, Will. Let me talk with your pa. Don't get your hopes up, though. Nothing could be done till after mud time, for sure."

Will sat in the chair that had become his place in the kitchen. "I have to be my own person, Ma. Don't you see? With or without a leg. I have to make my own life."

"One day at a time, Will. You've come far in the past months. Another month or two isn't too much to wait."

Will banged his crutch on the floor. "Another hour is too much! I love you and Pa, and everyone, and I love this house, but it isn't a refuge . . . it's a prison! You and Cassie do everything for me, and Pa and Simon and Nathan hardly look at me now. It's as if I no longer exist."

Ethan looked up from where he sat before the fire, where he was now piling pieces of kindling into small log houses. "Will, I look at you. I love you. Don't you love us anymore?"

"I love you very much, Ethan. But you can love someone and not be next to them every moment. Sometimes you need to have some distance between yourself and other people. Even those you love."

Ethan looked at his brother seriously. "If you go away, will you take your crutch with you?"

"Yes. I will take it with me."

"Will you take your animals?"

"No. I'll leave the animals. Will you take care of them for me?"

Ethan nodded. "Good care of them. Until you come back."

"Thank you, Ethan. I would like that." Will hugged Ethan and looked over at Ma, standing by the table. She looked sad, but she nodded. She understood.

"We'll talk to your pa after the excitement about statehood has simmered down."

CHAPTER 11

April 10

Spring at last! Yesterday I cut some pussy willow branches. I put them in water, and already they are sprouting tiny green leaves. The mud is deep, and it covers everything. Ma tries to have us clean our feet before we enter the house, but there is no hope of keeping all the dirt out. I have scrubbed the floor every day for weeks and know I will continue to do so for at least a week or two more. But the air smells fresh and sweet, birds are everywhere, and the trees have a haze of red or green or white around them, as leaves and flowers begin budding. I washed clothes early this morning and hung them over the blackberry bushes along the side of the house to dry for the first time since November. I sang to myself the whole time, I was so happy. As I did, Nathan drove up with Martha Bailey. They are now promised and will wed in October. She looked pretty in a new green petticoat, although I would think calico chilly this

early in the year. Nathan helped her off the wagon, and
they were on their way to the house when Will came out of
the privy. He called to them and waved, but as he did so
he slipped and fell on his face, right in the mud. I rushed
to help him, but he was indeed covered in the thick stuff.
Nathan and Martha tried but could not help laughing at
his appearance. Will did not laugh. He has not been to the
privy since but uses the chamber pot, as he did in winter.
I hope the ground dries quickly this year.

"He wants to go, John. He needs to feel he can take care
of himself. We have to let him go." Ma and Pa sat quietly at the pine table in the corner of the kitchen, keeping their voices as low as they could. But the house was
small; all who wished to hear could do so.

Pa's voice was clear. "He is of no use here, that is for
sure. Spending days whittling toys and sulking in the
corner is no good for him or for anyone else. But it is
not simple. I know Alice and Aaron have said they
would take him, but they do not know what that would
mean. He cannot reach high shelves. His stump aches
from the spring dampness. He slips when the floor or
dirt is wet or uneven. Here he sleeps near the kitchen.
At their home they have planned for him to sleep on the
second floor. But there is no railing on the stairs to the
second floor in their home. He would need help even
reaching the room they have in mind for him. Unless he
crawled and pulled himself up the stairs!"

"He wants this chance so much, John."

"He is getting along better with that crutch of his, but when he needs assistance, you and Cassie are always here."

"But Alice and Aaron are family too. And they do live near Dr. Theobold and others who might be able to help. His friend Sam is in Wiscasset too. Perhaps Sam can help him to meet other boys. He has seen almost no one but family since last September. He needs companions."

"Dreaming and hoping will not make life right itself. Will is a burden, Jess. No getting around it. And he is our son; our burden. God must be punishing us for something we have done, that He gave us a son like this. It would not be fair to pass that burden on to Alice and Aaron."

"But they have said they are willing. Perhaps for a short time?"

Ethan was playing with a small, carved wooden ball Will had made for him, while Cassie washed up the supper dishes. Suddenly she turned. "Will would not be a burden to Alice and Aaron if he had someone to help him," she said.

"Cassie, your pa and I were talking between ourselves," said Ma.

"But we all know Will wants to go to Wiscasset. Maybe Dr. Theobold can help him to walk again. He should have a chance!"

"What do you suggest, girl?" Her father's rough voice rose. "I suppose you have a solution?"

"I could go with him." Cassie talked quickly. "I know what his needs are, and he is used to my care. I could help Alice, too. With the two of us gone, Ma, you would not need as much help here. And Martha is close by and would value the chance to spend more time near Nathan if you did need assistance."

Ma and Pa looked at each other.

"It would only be until we know whether Will can use a new leg. Maybe for the summer. And we would not be far away. If we were a burden to Alice and Aaron, they could send us home."

Will came to the doorway of his small room. "Please. If Cassie were there, it would be easier."

Pa rose, looking from Will to Cassie and then back again. "All right! You may both go. But you are to come back if I hear you are any sort of trouble to Alice. And by the winter you must have found a place where you are not a burden, or you will both come back here."

Cassie and Will exchanged exultant glances. "Thank you, Pa," Will said, limping forward on his crutch to shake Pa's hand.

"You take care of each other, you hear? I am not so certain of the wisdom of this whole plan. But you will be with Alice, and she has said she wants you. Just remember, both of you, that your home is here. There are no miracles to be had in Wiscasset. Or anywhere." Pa turned and walked out the back door.

Ma got up and gave Cassie a hug. "You will both do just fine. Pa just doesn't want you to get your hopes up too high. And you will both be missed here, remember!"

Will grinned. "We will miss you, too, Ma. I promise to take good care of Cassie." He sat down and threw his crutch into the air and caught it. "Onward to Wiscasset!"

CHAPTER 12

May 2

I cannot sleep for excitement! Today Mattie and Tempe came to say good-bye, and each gave me two fine linen handkerchiefs they had embroidered to remember them by. I promised to write them all the town news. It is a time of new beginnings in so many ways! Maine's first governor has just been elected: General William King, from over to Bath. Pa is strutting proud, since he served under General King defending our coast during the War of 1812. And tomorrow Pa is driving Will and me to Wiscasset! I have prepared our summer clothing, but I fear it will not be adequate. In Wiscasset they no doubt dress more elegantly than in Woolwich. I do not wish us to be laughed at because of our clothing. Alice will know what more we may need and perhaps will even help me to sew any necessary garments. Will is excited and nervous, I can tell, but he says little. I pray Dr. Theobold can find a way for him to use a new leg. And I pray we

both will have a most excellent summer in Wiscasset.
After a winter spent in the kitchen and sickroom I am
anxious to be out and to see a little of the world. And to
be of help to Will, of course.

It wasn't a smooth journey, but both Will and Cassie were too excited to notice. Cassie sat up on the front seat with Pa. Will sat in back, propped between bundles of clothes and bedding, since he couldn't brace himself well enough with one foot to manage the high seat. Although it was May, and most of the mud was gone, the road was deeply pitted with the tracks of wagons that had trundled through on damper days.

Will and Cassie tried to see everything at once as they entered Main Street and drove by the half-finished Lincoln County Courthouse, the Congregational Church, the Green, the Lincoln and Kennebec Bank, and Turner's Tavern, and then made a left turn just before the block where many merchants had their shops. Will looked at the corner where he knew farmers would be selling their crops later in the season. It was now busy with sales of lambs and calves and seedlings for town gardens. He sat up straight, holding on to the side of the wagon, and stretched so he could see the river ahead. The life of a farmer was a dream of the past. He was here to find a new leg. And a new future.

Alice ran out to greet them as soon as she saw the wagon. "It is so wonderful that you both came," she exclaimed, helping Cassie and Will down from the wagon and hugging them so tightly that Will almost slipped on his crutch.

"Your ma wanted you to have these," Pa said, handing her two loaves of anadama bread and a pie made of dried apples. "She baked them especially for you and Aaron."

"And tell her we will love every bite," Alice enthused. "I have so missed seeing family through the long winter!"

"Well, I hear by next Thanksgiving you will have your own family," said Pa shyly as Alice blushed. "In the meantime, seems like I've brought you enough family to keep you occupied for the summer months."

"They are most welcome. I have been preparing for them since it was settled they could come." Alice helped Cassie and Pa unload the clothes and bedding. "Cassie and Will shall each have a side of the room next to Aaron's and mine. I even put a wardrobe in the middle so they could have some space of their own."

Pa shook his head. "You'll be spoiling them with city ideas. No harm in brothers and sisters sharing a room. How could families find space for everyone unless they did?"

"True enough, but I enjoyed fixing the room nice for them. Now, you all come in for something to eat and drink."

"No, thank you," said Pa. "Would like to, but I've got to get back. Ma will be waiting to hear these two are safely with you. And potatoes and wheat won't plant themselves. Remember, if there are any problems, you let us know, and I will be back to take them home."

"I am certain they will be just fine. Now, if you've got to be going, you go, because I want to get them settled before Aaron gets home from the store and starts calling for his supper."

Pa climbed back on the wagon and waved as he made his way back up Middle Street. As soon as his wagon vanished around the corner, Alice and Cassie each took a load of bedding into the house.

Will stood quietly and looked around. He was here. Wiscasset.

Two boys about his age were walking down the street toward him. One held a fishing pole, and the other carried a bucket of what Will assumed was bait, or perhaps even fish.

"Hello!" he called out. "Good fishing around here?"

The boys stopped and looked at him. Will stood tall, his crutch under his left arm, the left leg of his pants pinned up, and his blond hair tousled by the wagon trip.

"Do you fish in the river, or is there a stream or pond nearby?"

The boys stared at Will's pinned-up pant leg and fidgeted uncomfortably.

"Maybe sometime you could show me where the best spots are. I've come to stay with my sister."

The taller boy elbowed his companion, and the two of them started to run. As Will watched, they ran about a block and then slowed down and looked back, laughing and pointing.

Will turned and angrily pulled himself up the two granite steps to Alice's front door by balancing between his crutch and the iron rail.

Why could they not have at least stayed to talk?

But there must be lots of boys in Wiscasset. Sam was here. He wished Sam were with him now.

CHAPTER 13

May 4

We are really here, and settled in some! Alice has fixed a room especially for Will and me. It is on the second floor, which is difficult for Will, for he must take one step at a time, but I am here to ensure he doesn't slip. Perhaps after he gets his new leg, he will find the stairs easier. Alice has already shown me where everything is located. She has been a married woman and living in Wiscasset for over a year now. She knows everyone and everything. And with a baby to prepare for, I am sure there will be much to do this summer. It is so good to have someone with whom I can share my thoughts! Alice does not have my impatience; she is content with her life, as she says I must learn to be with mine. I will try. Will keeps his feelings to himself but seems pleased to be here. Being in town is different from being on the farm. The buildings are so close to one another, and there are so many people! But there are bright

*dandelions everywhere, just as there are at home. And
in Wiscasset I can help Will and learn from Alice and
perhaps even find a new life, too.*

"I promised Dr. Theobold we would visit him first
thing today," said Alice the next morning. Aaron had
left at dawn to open the store for early morning deliv-
eries of wood, greens, and home-woven fabrics from
local farmers. "The doctor needs to look at Will's leg to
see if it is healed enough to be fitted with a wooden
one. And I saw Sam on Main Street yesterday and
invited him to join us for supper tomorrow. I thought
you would be glad to see a familiar face, and he is anxious to see you both."

"How far is it to Dr. Theobold's home?" Cassie
asked. "Will has been inside all winter and has not
walked far with the crutch."

"I can do it, Cassie," Will said.

Alice hesitated a moment. "It is only a little over
two blocks. If you tire, Will, we can stop and rest along
the way. I have to learn what you can do."

Will stood up and glared at them both. "I will get
to where I need to go. I don't need two women worry-
ing over me." His crutch hit the floor hard as he walked
from the kitchen into the sitting room. "I will wait for
you on the steps." The front door closed loudly.

"Cassie, I'm sorry. Is Will strong enough to get there?"

Cassie nodded. "I think so. Especially since he fears

we might doubt him. His crutch is the problem. It rubs under his arm, and sometimes the arm blisters and bleeds." She hesitated. "He is used to my knowing and to my helping. But I think he is embarrassed for you to know."

"I did not realize it was so hard for him to walk. And I did not intend for my concern to distress him."

"Let us hope Dr. Theobold can make a difference," offered Cassie.

"He is a good man and a good doctor. It is too bad his wife is not well. She has a cough that kept her to home most of the winter. She is very delicate. But perhaps this warm weather will improve her health."

They left the house and walked slowly, admiring the budding trees and views of the river between the houses as they went.

The Theobold house was on a corner. As soon as they entered the yard, they were surrounded by what seemed an extraordinary number of barking dogs and running children. Will stood as squarely as he could, hoping none of the dogs would jump up and knock him over. Luckily none did, and after the doctor had come to the door and calmed down both dogs and children, it was clear there were only three dogs and two children. "This is Fred, who is eight, and Anne, who just turned four." Anne suddenly became shy and peeked out at them from behind her father's wide legs. "And these are our dogs: George Washington, John Adams, and Thomas Jefferson."

Cassie giggled as John Adams came up to sniff her. "Funny names for dogs!"

"We are a patriotic family. But my dear wife forbade my naming our children after presidents, so I had to be content to honor our dogs in that way." Dr. Theobold turned toward the house. "Now, come into my office and let me take a look at Will."

They followed the doctor toward the ell, the part of the house that connected the house to the barn. George Washington, John Adams, and Thomas Jefferson followed a few paces behind, as did Anne and Fred. Anne couldn't take her eyes off the place where Will's left leg should have been. Finally she tugged at his arm, almost pulling him down. "Where did you put your leg?"

Will looked down at her and smiled. It was the first time anyone had dared ask such a blunt question. And she was just Ethan's age. "It was hurt bad, and your pa had to cut it off."

"Will you grow another one? Starfish grow new arms when one is hurt."

"No. But your pa is going to help me walk better without growing a new one."

Anne nodded, and her long brown braids bounced. "My pa is a good doctor. He will help you walk better." She hopped three steps on one leg and then stopped. "But what happened to your leg? After Pa cut it off."

Will stopped. He had wondered the same thing, but had never dared ask.

"Our pa buried it," Cassie answered. "In our family's graveyard."

Will felt a tremendous wave of relief. Pa had not just thrown his leg on the compost pile, as he had imagined. It was where it should be. It was dead and could be mourned, but the rest of him was right here.

Anne smiled. "That was a good place."

Dr. Theobold leaned down to his daughter. "Young lady, I have to spend some time with these people now. You go with Fred and the dogs, or see if your mother could use some help with her roses." He straightened up. "My dear wife has a weakness for roses and has planted them all around our house. This is the time of year to remove winter mulches and ensure new branches are ready for spring. It takes her many hours, as her strength is not great, but when you see our yard in a month or so, I think you will agree her work is worth it. Beauty is like strength; it must be cultivated over time."

The doctor's office was a long, narrow room in the ell. Cassie walked over to the shelves that covered its walls and looked at the medical instruments, books, bottles of liquids and dried herbs, and tools like those Pa used for the animals or Will used to carve wood. The doctor's desk was covered with papers and a large leather-bound ledger, which lay open. He indicated that Cassie and Alice should sit on two chairs in the corner, and Will should sit on a low table in the center of the room.

Dr. Theobold spoke directly to Will, ignoring Cassie and Alice. "I'm glad you brought your sisters with you today, as after I examine you, we can share with them what we will be doing. But after this there should be no need for them to take the time to accompany you."

Cassie rose slightly, as if to speak, but Alice put out a hand to stop her.

Will looked at Cassie and then at the doctor. "I can come by myself. A man should be able to live his own life. He should be able to choose his own future."

"He should," agreed Dr. Theobold. "Although his choices may be directed by God, or by chance, or by whatever you might choose to call it. If you're walking in the woods, you may feel you're walking a straight line, but often the path you follow takes you left or right around trees, or even far in another direction to avoid a swamp or pond or bramble."

"True enough," agreed Will.

"Well, your path stopped at a large tree—perhaps even a large tree surrounded by a bramble. Now you will have to find a way around that tree. Or find another path altogether. Does that make sense to you?"

"It does, sir," Will said.

"Then, let us take a look at the stump of your leg and see what we can do to get you finding that path." He turned toward Cassie and Alice. "Ladies, perhaps you might enjoy talking to my wife about her roses while I examine Will."

Alice nodded and took Cassie's hand.

"But . . ." Cassie looked at Will. "I am here to take care of Will!"

Alice pulled her gently toward the door. "The doctor wants Will to have some privacy. He is old enough not to have womenfolk with him when a doctor is examining him. Come with me."

"But I've cared for Will all winter! He isn't embarrassed with me!" Cassie followed Alice outside.

"Then, perhaps Dr. Theobold is teaching Will that it is time for him to be so," advised Alice. "A man shouldn't be unclothed in the presence of someone not his wife."

Cassie looked at her sister in amazement.

"It is different in town than it was on the farm, Cassie. You and Will must learn that."

Half an hour later, when Will and the doctor walked around the back of the Theobolds' house, Cassie knew considerably more about roses and had established both Anne and Mrs. Theobold as new friends. She and Alice hardly heard Will calling to them.

"Alice! Cassie! I'm finished!" Will seemed to have grown taller even in that short time. And, in fact, the doctor had attached a piece of wood to the end of his crutch, so he did stand taller and straighter. "I'm to meet Dr. Theobold on Monday at the workshop of the cabinetmaker, Joshua Dann. He's going to make a new leg for me!"

Alice went toward him. "I can direct you to Mr. Dann's shop."

"And a harness maker is going to make a sort of bridle to hold the leg to my body. When it all fits well, then I can cover it with a trouser leg and a boot, and no one will see I have no leg!"

Dr. Theobold put his hand on Will's shoulder. "He will not be able to walk as he did before—a wooden leg, even one very well made, will not have a knee joint. The fitting, too, is difficult. The skin on his stump will have to thicken so it can bear the constant pressure of the padding between it and the leg. But I have no doubt that by autumn Will should be walking quite well."

"Autumn?" Will looked at him. "Will it take that long?"

"All things take time. You will need to learn how to walk again, this time with your new leg."

Will looked at the ground. His shadow fell clearly on the sand and bricks of the path. "The important thing is," Will said, pointing at his shadow, "that soon my shadow will again have two legs. I will not look like a gingerbread boy whose leg someone has nibbled."

Anne laughed. "You're not a gingerbread boy, Will. You're a man!"

"That's right," Will answered, straightening up. "I am."

CHAPTER 14

May 5

Since Will spoke with Dr. Theobold yesterday he has insisted on doing everything for himself. He struggled to pull on his trousers this morning and pin the extra leg up, and I am frustrated at not being permitted to assist him. Does he believe I was of such little use to him all winter, when every second sentence he uttered was one asking for my help? Despite his protests, I do not believe Will is finished needing people. But if he does not welcome my help, then I will find ways to assist Alice and, as she advised, let Will learn what he can and cannot do for himself. I am also beginning to see that I have much to learn from Alice and from Wiscasset about being a woman, much as Will is learning to be a man. It is a strange thought, since at home we were just a girl and a boy. But here the air seems full of possibilities.

"When do you get your new leg?" Sam took a big bite of the corn bread Alice had made to go with the evening's chowder. They were all sitting around the long pine table in the Deckers' kitchen. Cassie poured beer for the men, and lemonade for Alice and herself.

"I am to be measured for it early next week. But then it has to be made. I will not be running any races in the next week or so!" Will smiled. At home no one had mentioned his future or his lack of a leg except in terms of what he could not do. Here his lack of a leg was treated as a problem to be resolved, like a tooth that needed pulling.

"What will you do while the leg is being made?"

"I plan to look around Wiscasset. I have been here a few times before, but never long enough to really see it." Will took a big spoonful of the chowder. "This is wicked good chowder, Alice! We don't get fresh fish on the farm."

"Farm life depends on weather and time, and on the farmer's strength and endurance. Here you will find life and opportunities are measured by tides," said Aaron.

Sam took another bite of corn bread. "Mr. Wright, the silversmith I'm apprenticed to, does much work for sea captains and mariners just in from long journeys. They have coins jingling in their pockets and want something special for their mothers or sweethearts, or for themselves."

"What do you do for Mr. Wright?" Will asked,

spooning more chowder into his bowl from the tureen in the center of the table.

"Last fall, when I first came here, I just swept up, helped build fires, and kept the silver and clocks dusted. Then he began teaching me to clean the clocks and do minor repairs. The work often has to be done with tiny tools under a magnifier."

Will grinned. "A little different from forking manure out of your pa's barn, Sam!"

"For sure. This work is quiet and exact, and each clock a little different, so jobs are never the same twice."

"And you enjoy the work?" Cassie asked.

"I do. Someday I hope to build timepieces. Now that Maine is a state, more folks will be moving down east to live. I am hoping many will be needing clocks."

Aaron nodded. "Maine is just at the beginning of its prosperity. We've got land here, and our deep rivers give access not only to the seas, but to inland areas. It's a time of new beginnings, for sure."

"Is the mercantile business strong at John Stacy's store?" Sam asked Aaron.

"Sales always pick up in spring. More vessels are in and out of port, and people in the country are able to come to town for goods. Times are changing. Few women in town spin their own wool and weave their own cloth anymore; they buy calicoes and wools and muslins and even silks from us. And we also carry books and wines and glassware and fancy paper hangings for the walls of the big houses."

Will looked at Sam and Aaron. "I don't want to sit at a table and work under a glass all day like you, Sam, and I couldn't lift cartons and crates and climb ladders and fill wagons as you do, Aaron."

"So while we are looking around Wiscasset, we will also be looking for job possibilities for you," said Cassie. "You have a good brain, Will, and you are willing to work hard. There must be many trades you could learn."

"Will may choose to look by himself, Cassie," Alice said quietly. "There are many tasks we have to do inside the house."

"I don't mind her going with me," said Will. "Cassie hasn't seen much off the farm either. But"—he looked at her—"*I'll* be the one searching out a profession."

"There will always be more farmers than those in other occupations," Aaron said. "People will always need food. But farming isn't the only way to live. Here in the village there are people close by to be sociable with, a church you can walk to, and shops and doctors, banks and schools, within a few minutes' stroll. What more could someone want?"

Will didn't know what the future held for him here in Wiscasset, but he was certain of one thing. He was not going back to the farm to have Pa tell him again that he was a useless cripple.

CHAPTER 15

May 8

Will has gone to Mr. Dann's shop to meet Dr. Theobold and be measured for his new leg. He did not wish me to go with him. Since he left I have been unable to concentrate on helping Alice piece the quilt she is making in honor of Maine's statehood. I cannot calmly stitch vessels and pine trees while I am imagining Will falling in front of a horse's hooves, or slipping on filth in the streets, or getting lost and not finding the cabinetmaker's shop at all. If only I had gone with him! Perhaps I should have followed him without his knowing. But Alice bade me sit down and drink another cup of tea with her. Some mornings tea is all her stomach is able to settle, and I think she is glad of my company. But my mind is on Will, even as my hands are now on the piecing.

Walking in Wiscasset streets was very different from pacing Ma's kitchen floor. The dirt-and-stone road was slippery with manure from horses, dogs, oxen, and a small flock of sheep that a boy was heading back to the Green, where they should have been grazing. Will was not as steady on his crutch as he had bragged to Alice and Cassie, and he had to stop and rest every twenty steps or so.

At the corner of Water Street, the street nearest the Sheepscot River, he hesitated. The cabinetmaker's shop should be to his right. He turned into the river winds, which blew stronger than any he remembered on the farm, and braced himself for the final stretch. As he stepped out into the street, a large black dog raced toward him. Will tried to step aside, but the dog, dodging between wagons and tied horses, almost tripped him. Will was just regaining his sense of balance when he saw a boy running after the dog.

"Roddy!" the boy yelled as he followed the dog's course, weaving around oxen and horses and carts. "Roddy! Come back!"

Will stood uncertainly in the middle of the chaos. The other boy suddenly spun around, looking behind himself, and then turned to resume his search. Suddenly, despite both of their movements to avoid collision, he knocked against Will. Will turned on his foot, lost his balance, and fell heavily, twisting his ankle and catching his shirt on his crutch. The shirt ripped as Will hit the ground.

"I am *ever* so sorry! My dog's escaped again, and my father will be furious. Roddy chases Mrs. Pickle's sheep off the Green, and then Mrs. Pickle speaks harshly to my mum, and Mum cries, and Father said I'm to keep Roddy tied up, but he bit through the rope and . . ."

Will looked up at the boy in consternation. The dog was long gone. Will was sitting in the middle of a pile of horse manure, and already his ankle was swelling. "Would you help me up, please?"

"I didn't mean to knock against you. I never did." The boy reached down for Will's hand.

"And could you reach my crutch?"

"Oh, yes, of course." The boy looked confused for a moment and then handed Will the crutch.

Will was almost upright before he groaned. "My ankle. I've turned it badly. I don't think I can stand."

The boy helped him down onto a cleaner part of the road. They both looked around for help, but despite all the wagons and animals in the street, at the moment they were the only two people in sight.

"Do you know the shop of the cabinetmaker, Mr. Dann?" Will asked. "I was going there."

"It is just a few shops down." The boy pointed at a sign hanging above a shop only about thirty feet from them. CABINETMAKING, it said in gold above a painting of a ladder-back chair. JOSHUA DANN. "Perhaps I can fetch someone from there to help you?"

"Please," Will said with a nod. "Anyone who could help get me off the street before I am stomped on by a yoke of oxen!"

"Oh, yes, certainly! I'll be sharp." The boy took off, sprinting even faster than he had before. Will smiled despite the pain in his ankle and the embarrassment of sitting in the filthy street. Whoever this boy was, at least he was trying to rectify the damage he had caused. And he had not once said anything about Will's leg or blamed him for falling or laughed at him.

The boy was back quickly enough with a short, round, ruddy-faced man wearing a long apron. "Here, you see, I've brought someone," he announced proudly. "This is Mr. Dann."

"You must be Will," Mr. Dann said. Will nodded in confirmation. "Here, Paul, you lift him from the right side and I'll take the left. Cross your hands . . . like so . . ." He demonstrated. "We'll make a chair of our hands to carry Will down to my shop. Dr. Theobold is going to join us there, so he'll take a look at that ankle.

"You carry your crutch," Mr. Dann said, handing it to Will. "Now . . . ready, Paul? Let us lift him up."

The cabinetmaker's shop smelled of the dust of pine and maple and other woods, and of pungent varnish and oils. Despite the pain in his ankle, the filth on his clothes, and the embarrassment of being carried by two people he did not know, Will inhaled deeply. This shop had the familiar smell of his wood carvings multiplied many times. Mr. Dann and Paul set him down on a low stool near the door. Will ran his fingers over the inlay on the leg of the small table next to him. He looked up at Mr. Dann. "You made this?" he asked.

Mr. Dann nodded. "I did."

"What wood is it?"

"A dark mahogany inlaid with a lighter shade."

Will touched it gently. "It is beautiful. I have never seen anything like it."

"I learned to inlay mahogany where I apprenticed in Philadelphia. Several cabinetmakers there do fine work. Here there is little call for it. Inlay work takes expensive wood and many hours. People in Maine who can afford to pay for such work order furniture from Europe, or from New York or Philadelphia. Most of what I do is much simpler." He gestured toward several pine chests and tables and a large wardrobe in the corner of his shop. "But when I have time, I try to craft a few pieces that are special."

"Are you going to be all right, then?" Paul looked from one to the other. "If there is no need for me at the moment, I really must find Roddy."

"Thank you—Paul—for everything," Will said with a smile.

"For knocking you down and keeping you from walking, you should say." Paul reached out his hand. "My name is Paul North. My parents and I moved here from London last August. And I have a bad habit of moving too fast and not looking where I am going."

"I'm Will Ames from Woolwich. I am staying with my sister and her husband, Aaron Decker, on Middle Street."

"I must search out Roddy before he terrorizes all the sheep in Wiscasset." Paul turned toward the door. "But I would like to come and see if you are all right. May I call on you, Will? Perhaps in a few days?"

Will grinned. "Stop anytime. As long as you keep Roddy at a bit of a distance so I can stay upright."

"I shall. I promise." Paul opened the door and dashed out.

"A nice young fellow, but wherever he is, he is always on the verge of going somewhere else," said Mr. Dann. "His father bought the lumberyard over on the point last year. They live a little north of town, past the old graveyard."

Before Will had a chance to ask anything more, the door opened again and Dr. Theobold appeared. He took in the situation at once.

"Well, I see you arrived before me, Will, and I suspect in more dramatic fashion."

Will pulled his torn shirt closed. "I slipped a bit on the street. I've hurt my ankle."

Dr. Theobold got down on his knees, removed Will's boot, and touched the ankle and foot gently. Will winced. "You've given that ankle a nasty twist, but it appears you have not broken anything, thank goodness. That would have put you in a difficult situation. But you will not be able to stand safely on that ankle for a few days."

Will's face fell. "I hoped to be measured for my new leg."

"I see no reason why you should not be! You are here and so are we. Joshua, can you take the measure of this young man's leg while he is sitting down, or shall we stand him up?"

"Leave him where he is for now while I get my rule," Mr. Dann said. "When I am almost certain I have got the correct measurements, we can prop him up for a few moments while I check."

"Then, I will have my new leg soon!"

"Only if you promise not to twist it as badly as you have this other one," Dr. Theobold advised. He watched as the cabinetmaker measured the length of Will's leg and foot, and of his stump, to ensure both legs would be the same height. "How long should it take for you to make Will's leg?"

"Close to two weeks," Mr. Dann replied. "I am in the middle of several other jobs that need finishing up. This is the first leg I have made, and I consider it a personal challenge. I want to make sure it is done right."

"Craft the leg so the stump can fit down into it. There needs to be space for a leather lining and some padding so it does not rub too hard."

Mr. Dann nodded and took additional measurements.

That night Will dreamed of a room full of mahogany wooden legs with inlays showing its blood vessels and nerves. The biggest leg stood in the center of the room like a pedestal. On it was a crystal vase of dark red roses.

CHAPTER 16

May 8, evening

I should have insisted I go with Will this morning! Dr. Theobold half carried him back to the house today. His shirt that I had stitched so carefully was torn, he was filthy from the streets, and his ankle was swelling like a cow's udder at milking time. Alice seemed little concerned after we were assured his ankle was not broken; the muscles have just been bruised. But for now Will cannot get to the second floor of the house, and I have spent the better part of today cleaning his clothes and carrying his bedding down to the kitchen to make a place for him there until his ankle is stronger. I think I should also sleep downstairs, in case he has need of me in the night, but Alice says I need not. Will is so full of stories of some boy from London who knocked him down, and a cabinetmaker's shop full of furniture, that he hardly seems to notice his ankle. Thank goodness I am here to make sure someone cares for him. He

certainly has not done well caring for himself thus far.
If Pa were to know, he'd be taking us both back to
Woolwich right quick. And he'd be just to do so. Perhaps
Alice is correct: All men need a woman to watch out for
them. Although if that is so, then who watches out for
women, other than God?

"Cassie, Will is doing fine. He has his wood if he wants
to carve, and he has a book to read. He has no need for
anything else right now. You and I could walk down by
the wharves and breathe some fresh air." Alice paced
restlessly as Cassie put a pitcher of water next to Will's
pallet on the floor. Will ignored them both.

"Will, I left you some more water, in case you
should be thirsty."

Will nodded.

"Is the book that good?" Cassie asked. Paul had
been bringing Will books to keep him amused while his
ankle healed. He had brought this latest one just last
night.

Will looked up. "After I finish, you must read it too,
Cassie! Washington Irving has written a wonderful story
about a man who falls asleep for twenty years."

"The way you have been sleeping recently, that
could be you," Cassie countered. "I know you are to rest
your ankle, but the doctor did not tell you to sleep all
the time!"

"It must be the river air." Will grinned at her. He

didn't mention the candles Aaron had been bringing him each night so he could continue reading long after the others had gone to sleep. "You go and walk with Alice. I'll be fine here, and you have not been out since I hurt my ankle."

"I am waiting to see Wiscasset with you."

"Well, go with Alice and enjoy it for yourself. The doctor told Alice she should be walking more since the baby quickened." Alice had shared the excitement of feeling the baby's first movements and since that moment had put thoughts of her child ahead of all else. Will turned back to his book.

Cassie sat down next to him. "How can you sit so quietly for hours? Last year at this time you were helping Pa shear the sheep or planting corn and beans. You rarely rested."

Will looked at her. "That was last year, Cassie."

They both thought of the farm chores Will could no longer do. Will broke the silence. "And a year ago Ma was always looking to see where you had hidden so you could avoid helping her ready the house for summer."

Cassie made a face back at him. That had been when she was a little girl. Life had changed for both of them since last year.

Alice sighed. "Will is teasing, Cassie. But if you'll not leave the house, then at least let us bake some extra bread. It will save us time tomorrow morning."

Cassie went over to the cupboard to get the large wooden dough bowl. As she walked back to the table, she paused at the back door to look at the lupine beginning to bloom in the yard. "Alice, do you ever miss the fields and the farm?"

"Sometimes. When I see the flowers here and remember the fields of wildflowers near home. And when the smells and sounds of the streets remind me how quiet it seemed on the farm. But Aaron and I have a good life. I knew when I married that my life would be different from Ma's. Aaron has always lived in town and doesn't know country life. But he is a fine man. I knew that from the first time I met him at his cousin's barn raising." The color rose in Alice's face, as though she were remembering.

"At home life was simple," Cassie said. "Everything we needed was right there, and everyone knew what they had to do to keep the farm going." She reached deep into the wooden flour bin. "At home going to services on Sunday was the only regular time to see people. Here men, and even women, sail to Portland or Boston with hardly a thought. And there are laces and spices and books and perfumes in John Stacy's store that I could never have imagined. Possibilities for what a person could do in life seem limitless here."

"Like the books Paul has brought from the Social Library for Will to read. We had no books like that at home." Alice looked down at her belly. "My son or daughter will be able to read books and hear music and know about more things than the cycles of the moon and the harvest. Who knows where life may take this child?"

Cassie put the flour into the bowl and turned to get the salt. She looked out the door again and went out into the yard. In a minute she was back, carefully holding three long-stemmed white balls of feathery dandelion seeds. "Remember when we were little?" she said as she handed one to Alice and one to Will. "We used to say that if we could blow all the seeds into the air with one breath, then our wish would come true."

"I haven't done that in years," Alice said. She carefully put a linen cloth over the mixing bowl, took a deep breath, and blew the white seeds all over the kitchen. "Now your turn. But you have to sweep up after!"

Cassie closed her eyes and then opened them and blew as hard as she could. She turned to Will. "You now, Will."

Will looked up from his book. He, too, blew dandelion seeds all over the kitchen. "What did you wish for, Alice?"

"That my baby be well born and my birthing easy. That is really two wishes, but there were a lot of seeds on that dandelion!"

Cassie laughed.

"And your wish, Cassie?"

"I wished to know my purpose in life," Cassie said.

Alice looked at her. "But you do know it! Like the purpose of every woman, yours is to marry and care for your husband and children, and ensure that your home is filled with love and faith and caring. And that is a purpose easier to say than to accomplish."

"But sometimes I feel caring for one family will not be enough. I want to do more!"

Alice laughed. "Someday you will find caring for one family will take every hour of your every day, Cassie. There is no time for a woman to do more than that. What did you wish for, Will?"

"I wished you would both leave me alone so I could finish this book!"

CHAPTER 17

May 21

Tomorrow Will is to get his new leg. His ankle is better,
though still weak. Dr. Theobold will come for him in
the morning. I wish I could be there when they fit the
leg. I am curious about how it shall work, and I hope it
enables Will to walk as well as he is confident it will. I
have had no dreams in the past days except of pails of
sand and soapy water. Alice's work in Wiscasset is the
same as Ma's in Woolwich. We have been scouring the
walls and floors, washing bedding, and cleaning the
pantry of winter supplies. Soon enough it will be time to
start replacing those foodstuffs for next winter. The
work it takes to keep a house in order seems one unend-
ing circle of sameness. I wonder if I shall be back at
home by winter, or whether perhaps I could stay here?
Ma will have Martha to help her by then, and Alice will
need assistance after her baby is born. Alice says the
Wiscasset census counted more than two thousand

*people. With so many people, surely both Will and I can
find places to be of use. If I have to scrub floors, then
perhaps at least I could scrub floors to be walked on by
people with different ideas, who have traveled to different places.*

The leg was made of pine, and it did not look as Will had
hoped. "It isn't shaped like a leg," he pointed out quietly.

"No. But it is shaped to support you." Dr. Theobold
pointed to the bottom of the leg, which was at a right
angle to the vertical piece. "This piece is made to fit
into a boot; perhaps a little wider than the boot you are
wearing on your right foot, but a shoemaker can easily
make up the difference."

"But it is not as long as my foot," Will pointed out.
In fact, the pine foot was only a few inches long.

"No." Mr. Dann came over and pointed. "But on a
real leg your ankle and knee joints allow you to move
your foot up and down. They make your gait regular
and enable you to go up hills or climb steps. With an
artificial leg there is no way to control joints, so there
are none. If I were to make the foot longer, it would get
in your way, since it will always be in the same position."

Will nodded slowly. He hadn't thought of that.

Dr. Theobold put his hand on Will's shoulder. "You
will have to learn to use it, just as when you were a baby
you learned to walk. Let's see if the bucket top Mr.
Dann has made will fit you well."

As Will took down his trousers, the carving he had been working on fell out of his pocket. Mr. Dann picked it up.

"Is this your work, Will?"

"I was trying to carve my sister Alice's face. It is a rough attempt." Will reached for the piece of wood.

"Do you do much carving?"

"I like to whittle. I made dozens of animals for my little brother last winter. Working with wood helps pass the time. But this is the first face I've attempted."

Mr. Dann took the little carving closer to the store window. "You have an excellent sense of the wood; you have captured the movement of your sister's hair." He turned back. "You have a talent, Will. Have you thought of learning woodworking?"

"The whittling is just to amuse myself. Most farm boys whittle."

"But most farm boys do not have your hand or your eye. Have you seen this work, Doctor?"

"No," said Dr. Theobold, taking the carving from Mr. Dann and examining it. "But I can see what you mean. Clearly the boy knows how to handle a knife."

"Thank you, sir." Will reached out for the carving. "The face is not yet finished." He sat awkwardly on the edge of the chair. He hoped no one would walk into the shop while he was wearing only his short summer drawers. "Nor has my leg been fitted."

"Then, we will indeed return to the task at hand," said Mr. Dann, smiling.

Mr. Dann had made a deep carving in the top of the pine leg, like a cutout for a pegged beam in a barn. But the peg that was to go in this opening was Will's stump. Will supported himself on Dr. Theobold's shoulder and carefully fit his body into the leg. Although the pocket had been lined with soft brown moose leather, the leg still rubbed.

"There is no avoiding that," said the doctor as he looked carefully at the stump and leg. "We can add a little linen to the bucket." That was softer, but only a little.

Will quickly identified another problem the men were too discreet to point out: Even his shortest summer drawers were too long to be worn with this leg. The drawers got caught between his stump and the wooden bucket on the top of the leg. Cassie would have to make him another pair, with a shorter left leg.

"You need to have control of the leg, so the fit needs to be close. If we allow too much space for padding, then the leg will not be tight. On the other hand, if it is too tight, it will chafe and you will get blisters and sores on your stump, as if you were wearing shoes that were too tight."

Will moved a little in the bucket. "Maybe it will be all right once I get used to it."

"Your stump will have to become callused, like the

bottom of a foot worn without shoes in summer becomes hardened," Dr. Theobold explained.

Will thought suddenly of how it felt to wiggle his toes in mud or to feel summer sun warming his whole body. He would never feel those things again. Despite his blinking, his eyes filled with tears.

"I told you it wouldn't be easy, Will," Dr. Theobold said quietly.

Mr. Dann patted Will's shoulder and added some more gauzy cotton to the padding of the leg's bucket. Then he attached the moose leather harness that the saddler had made to hold the leg on.

Will had already given up thoughts of marching through the streets of Wiscasset today on his new leg. He was now wondering whether he would even be able to put it on and take it off by himself.

Maybe Cassie had been right; would he always need her assistance?

Just then the door opened. A big man, more elegantly dressed than most in Wiscasset, entered.

Will moved as quickly as he could to a space in back of the table. His face flushed. His body was exposed more than was seemly.

"Good afternoon, Captain Morgan," said Mr. Dann, bowing slightly to the gentleman. "How may I help you this beautiful day?"

"I am here to see your work," said the gentleman, examining the inlaid mahogany tables near the front of the store. "You may have heard I am having another vessel built, over to Tinkham's Shipyard."

"I had heard that, sir," answered Mr. Dann.

Dr. Theobold helped Will move farther back into the shop and adjust his trousers.

"Dr. Theobold, are you here to purchase some furniture?" asked the captain.

"Not today," he replied. "Mr. Dann was doing some custom work for Will Ames. I am here to advise them."

"And how goes it?"

His body now covered, Will grinned and limped forward a step or two with his crutch to demonstrate his new leg. "It is not inlaid mahogany, but it is mighty good cabinetry, sir."

Captain Morgan smiled. "I can see that." He turned to Mr. Dann. "I, too, am here about some custom work. I have always had the captain's quarters and figureheads for my vessels designed in Boston. But now that we are no longer part of Massachusetts, I would like to have the work on a State of Maine brig done here. Do you have the skills and time to take on such a project?"

"A figurehead, no," replied Mr. Dann. "My skills are not in that sort of work. But the quarters I think I could do. If you give me measurements and some idea of what you would like, I could draw up some designs to see if they would suit you."

"Excellent."

Dr. Theobold took Will's arm and helped him walk

slowly toward the door. "We thank you, Joshua, for your time. Will and I will let you know how he is getting on."

"You are quite welcome," said Mr. Dann. "I look forward to seeing you both." He turned toward his new customer. "If you have the time, Captain, perhaps we could go over those measurements now?"

As he walked slowly down the street, leaning on the doctor's arm, Will asked, "What is a figurehead, Doctor?"

"It is a carving of a person or an animal, more than life-size, attached to a sailing vessel under the bowsprit. Sailors say it brings luck to a ship if the figurehead has the right spirit."

Will's mind filled with the idea of a carving larger than a person. "Are there many men who do such carvings?"

"Not in Maine. Figureheads you'll see on vessels in our harbor have been done in Boston or Philadelphia, I believe," answered the doctor. "But I am not an expert on such things. When you next see Mr. Dann, perhaps you could ask him."

"I will," said Will, hardly noticing the blisters that were beginning to form on his stump where it rubbed the new leg. "And I'll look more closely at vessels when I am next down at the harbor."

CHAPTER 18

June 2

After more than a week of practicing within the house, Will is now walking slowly back and forth on Middle Street. I accompanied him at first, but he was embarrassed to have a girl for assistance, even if the girl was his sister. In a town such things can be seen by the world. If we were back at the farm, I cannot think it would have been important to him. His new leg is paining him, and at night he bathes his stump in willow water to keep down the redness and swelling. The leather harness to hold the leg on functions rather like gallows—or as a gentleman would say, braces—do to keep up a pair of high stockings. But even though the harness is made of softened moose leather, it chafes Will's waist and causes him much discomfort. He has tried wearing it both over and under his shirt, but either way is awkward. Sam came to see him this morning, and now his new friend, Paul, is here. It is good he has

*two friends who neither cater to him, nor ask him to do
things that are impossible. I miss Mattie and Tempe and
look forward to their letters. But they are too busy with
cooking and cleaning and taking care of little brothers
and sisters to write often. They say all is the same in
Woolwich. I help Alice in the kitchen, but without seeds
to plant and cows to milk and chickens to feed and butter to churn, there is less to do than on the farm. I had
thought Will's needs would fill my life, but he is deter-
mined they will not, so I must find other projects or
people to fill my hours.*

Will had been walking twenty minutes without a break.
"I would like to rest awhile," he admitted to Paul.
"Could we sit on the steps for a few minutes? If you
would like to go somewhere else, you know I would not
mind."

"I came to see you, not to test out the strength of
your leg," Paul answered easily as they sat on the top
granite step outside the Deckers' house.

"Wiscasset must seem very quiet for you after living
in London." Will reached into his trouser pocket and
pulled out his carving of Alice and a small chisel.

"Quiet? Yes. But there are many things to do here,
too. In London I was required to study most of the
time, and wear elegant clothes and be polite all of the
time. Here I go to school in the winter, but in summer
I am free to fish or row or go swimming." Paul looked

at Will. "Perhaps you could swim without your leg. The hulk of an old frigate, the *United States,* has been stripped and left to rot on the mudflats near Payson's Wharf. We boys dive off it. You might have trouble climbing onto the vessel. But I'll wager you could swim!"

"I used to swim in a pond near the farm," Will recalled. "The cool water felt mighty good after a hot summer's day in the fields. But river water is salt, and colder, and the currents run stronger."

"It is not as cold in places where the tide goes all the way out; the sun heats up the mudflats, and they warm the shallow water when it comes back on the tide. Someday I will show you."

"You had lessons in London? Did you go to school, then?"

"Well, not school precisely. I had a tutor to help prepare me for Cambridge, the university my father attended. I have the same arrangement here, actually, only the tutor in London was devoted to just my cousins and me."

"You have a tutor in Wiscasset?"

"Reverend Packard."

"The minister?"

"He is a graduate of Bowdoin College and proud of it. In winter he teaches a few boys who are preparing for Bowdoin or for one of the other colleges. Only, no one mentions Harvard or Yale when he is around. For the reverend Bowdoin is the only school worth attending."

"It is in Maine!"

"True. And well respected. Men come from all over New England to attend there. But it is not the only college in the States."

"You are planning to go to college, then?"

"My father wants me to become a lawyer. I don't know what I want. But I have no great interest in the trades, or any talent at skilled labor such as Sam is learning. So I may as well study my Latin and Greek until I decide what is right for me. What will you do?"

"I was going to farm, until the accident." Will's voice was steady. As the months passed, it was easier to talk about it. "Pa said a cripple is of no use on a farm. He made me so angry; I wanted to prove to him I could farm. I thought perhaps I could with my new leg. But now I know he was right. I miss the smells of the fields, and the animals, and the sound of the wind through the wheat. But farming would be too difficult. How could I keep my balance while steadying a plow or chasing a hog? Now I'm considering other professions."

"Certainly! Not everyone in the world works a farm!"

"But I would be bored staring through a glass at tiny clockworks all day, as Sam does. Being a mariner would offer the same challenges as being a farmer. A mariner must lift and carry and work quickly in emergencies. If I could see a point in learning your Latin and Greek, I suppose I could do it. But all the books I want to read are in English!"

Paul grinned. "There are other books that are interesting. But the truth is that most can be read in English translations. And if you have no interest in becoming a professor or lawyer or doctor, there is no reason to spend your nights trying to read Greek letters by candlelight."

"You do it."

Paul shrugged. "Until I find something that suits me better, I do." He looked down at the work in Will's hand. "That is a terribly good likeness of Alice. If I could whittle the way you can, why, I might decide to be a great sculptor instead!"

Will laughed. Carving was as much a part of him as his nose. He seldom thought about it. "I cannot see a sculptor making a living in Wiscasset. Even if I could be one!"

"Wiscasset is not the world."

"Perhaps not, but it is plenty big for me. Come; I'm ready to take a few more circles around Middle Street." Will righted himself, then tucked the wooden face back into his pocket, and he and Paul started down the street.

Just then the two boys Will had seen on his first day in Wiscasset rounded the corner. "Who are those two?" Will asked quietly. "I see them often in the streets, but they avoid me. Or laugh at me."

"Davey and Thom Pendleton, from down on

Washington Street. Their pa is a mariner and to sea much of the time. Watch out for both of them; they can be trouble."

"Hey!" called out the taller of the boys. "Hey, Paul!"

"Davey," acknowledged Paul.

"Who's your hobbling friend?"

Will flushed.

Paul answered calmly. "This is Will Ames. He is staying with their sister and her husband for the summer."

"We've been watching him limping along. We've been wagering as to when he will fall, haven't we, Thom?"

"Figure he won't make it to Main Street without leaning on someone's arm. Why are you hanging around a cripple, Paul? Boys are playing ball up on the Green."

Will stopped.

"I have no desire to play ball today." Paul kept walking, indicating Will should do the same. "Some other time, perhaps."

"We've been down to the pier for a swim. Guess that would be too far for your crippled friend to limp."

"I can walk any place I choose to," Will's voice was louder than he thought it would be.

"Then, maybe one of these days we'll be seeing you down at the pier," Thom said as they came abreast of each other. Suddenly, without warning, he reached out and kicked Will's good leg. Will crashed down in a heap, while Thom and Davey raced for the end of the street.

"Hey—stop!" Paul raced after them, but they were too fast. He turned and ran back to Will. "I told you those two were trouble. Are you all right?"

"My body is fine." Will's face was red with anger. "Give me a hand up?"

Paul reached down and helped Will to his feet.

"Where did you say this pier was—the place we're going to swim? I had better start practicing."

CHAPTER 19

June 26

Every day Will walks farther and more smoothly. His stump is now accustomed to pressure from the leg. I have made him two new pairs of drawers that do not get in the way of either his new leg or the harness. Over the leg he can wear trousers, as he used to, although he had new boots made to fit both his growing foot and his shorter wooden one. Wiscasset is beautiful in the summer. Afternoon sea breezes off the river keep the town cooler than our farm would be in June, but not chilly. Will has made a habit of walking down to the wharves in the afternoon and watching the vessels in the harbor. Mrs. Theobold's rose garden has been blooming for a week now, and every time I see it, there are different blossoms. I have decided to make a patchwork quilt with a different rose on each patch. Alice thinks that a splendid idea and has agreed to help me find the right materials. She thinks the quilt is to be saved for use after my marriage someday. But I see no reason to wait to enjoy it. Tomorrow we are all going to take a holiday and pick strawberries north of Wiscasset. On the farm picking strawberries would be a chore, the first step toward preserving fruit for winter. Here jams and jellies are available at all times in the mercantile, and strawberry picking is seen as an excuse to be out of doors. On a farm there is no need for such excuses!

They left their beds as the sun was rising, while sea mists still covered the town. Alice prepared tea for herself and coffee for Cassie, Will, and Aaron, and cut chunks of bread and sage cheese for breakfast.

"I am longing for some sweetness," she confided to Cassie. "Sometimes I get weary with eating fish and venison and beef. And the tart sweetness of fruit is so different from the sweetness of molasses or maple syrup."

"Will there be enough strawberries so we can make jam for winter?" Cassie took a bite of the green cheese, relishing the fresh taste of the sage. It would be fun to make jam with Alice. They had done it many times in the past under Ma's direction, but now they were sharing kitchen tasks like two women friends would.

"I hope so. I asked Aaron to gather all the tins and baskets he can find in the shed so we can load ourselves down with berries. And I saved a cone of sugar for making the jam."

"Is the way long? I am concerned for Will."

"He would be more upset if we were to go without him. The field is not far, but the land there is uneven. It will not be easy for him. And picking the berries may be even more difficult, since he cannot bend down easily."

"He can sit on the ground and pick."

"That is what I thought. And we will all be with him, should he need assistance."

Will joined them, carrying two baskets. "Aaron said we were to carry baskets. Are these from the back hall what you want, Alice?"

"The very ones. Now, have some breakfast, and we'll be off as soon as Aaron is ready."

By six thirty they were organized, complete with baskets and buckets, and heading toward the field. "Please, could we stop for a moment to see the Theobolds' roses?" Cassie asked.

Alice smiled. "Their home is not far off the way. You run ahead, and we will join you in a moment." She shifted her baskets slightly to better balance herself. "We'll take the back path past the old cemetery, up the Alna Road."

Dr. Theobold and the children were in their yard. Despite the hour, Fred had already gathered a large bouquet of roses. "Oh," Cassie said, "how beautiful." Fred smiled and held them out for her to smell. "I think heaven must smell like roses." She looked around. "Where is Mrs. Theobold?"

"Ma is not well again, Cassie," said Fred. "That's

why we're picking the roses. To take inside so she can have them near her bed."

Cassie looked at the doctor in concern. "I had hoped she would be better by now!"

"I wish it were so, Cassie. Sometimes even a doctor cannot make things right." He hesitated. "My dear wife is trying very hard, but she has never been strong. I am glad the roses can make her smile, even if she cannot walk to see them herself."

"May I help in any way?"

He looked at the baskets she was carrying. "You look as though you're on your way to a beautiful day strawberrying. Perhaps, if it is not too much trouble, you could take Fred and Anne with you?" His children wiggled in excitement. "I need to stay close to home, and the children should be out of doors, enjoying this fine June weather. Their mother would be pleased to know they were with you."

"Then, they will come," Cassie said. She turned to Fred and Anne. "Do you think you could find any baskets or buckets to put strawberries in? You could pick some to bring back to your ma."

"I'll get baskets," called Fred, running toward their barn.

Dr. Theobold suddenly looked tired. "Thank you and your family very much. A day outside town picking strawberries is just what the children need. And perhaps a day of quiet is what my wife and I need."

Before Cassie could say anything more, Fred came running back, carrying an armload of baskets.

"We will be off, then," said Cassie, herding the children toward the road, where the rest of the family was waiting for them. "I promise to bring them safely back to you, Dr. Theobold."

He waved. "I have no doubt. If only the world were as simply planned. You are too young to know how difficult it can be." He looked up and saw Will waiting for Cassie.

"But no. You *do* know how life can change in directions we do not wish." The doctor sighed and went toward his house.

"Life can change, can't it?" Cassie said to Fred and Anne. "But new roads can lead to exciting places too."

"Like strawberry fields?" asked Anne.

"Exactly. Like strawberry fields."

CHAPTER 20

July 6

Mrs. Theobold is now very poorly. Her cough is heavy, and her head pains her so she cannot raise it from her pillow. I helped the doctor bathe her body, which was damp with the heat of July and her fever, and then held the bowl for him while he bled her to try to reduce her fever and put her body back in balance. It seems logical that too much blood should cause someone to have fever and a fast pulse, and yet the cure does not seem to be helping Mrs. Theobold. Poor little Anne and Fred are very patient, but it is clear they do not understand why their mother is unable to play or make their supper. I left some chowder on the fire for them all, hoping Mrs. Theobold would be strong enough to take some. The doctor has asked me if I can come again when he has patients to see in the country, as he cannot take his children with him or leave them with his sick wife. Tomorrow Will is going to have the doctor check the skin

on his stump to ensure it has not become too inflamed.
I will go with him and perhaps take some cakes for the
children.

"Which do you think they would want?" Will asked
Cassie as he looked at the row of wooden animals he
had carved since he'd been in Wiscasset. "Ethan loved
the horses, but I think perhaps Anne would like a cat."

"And a dog for Fred. That one looks a little like
George Washington." Cassie pointed to the dog on the
end of the line, his ears and head alert.

"It does. Fred might like that one," said Will, putting the cat and the dog in different pockets. "Dr.
Theobold has helped us so much and has asked for such
little payment. I hope he won't mind my bringing the
children small gifts."

"I am certain he will not," assured Cassie. "I've taken
food to them before. This is a hard time for the family.
Can you imagine what it would have been like if Ma
had been so sick?"

Will shook his head. "Dr. Theobold does not seem
able to heal his own wife."

"He bleeds her and gives her drinks to bring down
the fever and quiet her cough, but she continues to
weaken."

Anne and Fred Theobold were in their yard. Their
roses still bloomed, but many blossoms were now hanging low with the heat and drought. George Washington,

John Adams, and Thomas Jefferson were chasing sticks the children threw across the yard. All five ran to welcome Cassie and Will.

"It's a good thing I'm now sturdier on my leg," said Will, grinning as John Adams jumped up and tried to lick his face. "Down, boy!" He turned to the children. "I've brought you each something. Which pocket do you think they are in?"

"That one!" Both Anne and Fred answered, each pointing to different pockets.

"You're both right!" Will reached into his pockets and pulled out the cat and the dog, which he handed ceremoniously to the children. "The cat is for you, Anne, and the dog for Fred."

"Oh!" Anne gave Will a big hug. "She is cunning! Thank you! This is my favorite cat from now on."

"This is pretty nice, all right," agreed Fred, looking his dog over. "Look, Pa," he called as Dr. Theobold came out of his medical room and walked slowly toward them. "See what Will has given us!"

The doctor took a good look, carefully examining both the dog and the cat. "I had forgotten your carving. These are well done, Will."

"Thank you, sir."

"You have great skill with your hands," the doctor added, handing the small cat back to Anne. "Now, come with me so I can check that leg of yours."

"I've brought some cakes for the children," said

Cassie as Fred and Anne bounced up and down beside her, trying to lift the cloth covering her basket. "I'll put them in the kitchen for you."

"Thank you, Cassie," said Dr. Theobold.

"Pa, can we have a cake?" pleaded Anne.

"One each," agreed the doctor. "Cassie, be sure to put the rest of the cakes above the counter in the kitchen. So that," he said, looking at his children, "the dogs won't be able to get them."

Cassie handed one cake each to Fred and Anne, and they all headed for the kitchen as Dr. Theobold and Will went into the medical room.

The doctor's room was cool. Will walked to the low table where the doctor usually examined him, and unfastened his trousers.

"Your stump is doing well," the doctor pronounced. "You must continue to use the willow water, though, to keep the swelling down in this heat."

"It has been rubbing more the past few days," Will admitted.

"Then, you may need to reduce the layers of cloth you have between your leg and the leather cup," advised the doctor. "In summer the body swells, and you could blister your stump more quickly than you would think. I have had to cut wedding rings off women's fingers that were so swollen with the heat that the ring became a tourniquet." Dr. Theobold paused a moment. "Let me take a look at your hands."

Surprised, Will held them out. "There is nothing wrong with my hands, sir."

"Your hands are strong, Will."

"From farming. And whittling. And supporting myself on the crutch."

"You have skill with a knife. Not everyone can use a tool with the delicacy you used when you carved those animals. Have you ever thought of other uses for a knife?"

Will shook his head.

"Surgeons have to be good with their hands too. Do you mind the sight of blood?"

"No." Blood was a common sight on a farm.

"Have you ever thought of becoming a doctor?"

Will looked around the room at all of the surgical instruments and bottles and dried herbs stored there. "You have to know a lot of things to be a doctor."

"True. But all professions require learning. The learning is just of different types."

Will thought of Paul studying Latin and Greek.

"Does a doctor have to learn foreign reading?"

"Most do. There are different ways of becoming a doctor. In Europe doctors like my father trained at universities and studied old medical texts in Greek and Latin and new ones in French and German and English. I grew up in this country, where there were few schools of medicine and no money in my family to send me abroad, so I apprenticed to my father, and he taught me what he knew. I also read the journals and books published every year telling of new developments and ideas in medicine."

"If I wanted to become a doctor, could I be an apprentice to you?"

"That could be the beginning. That would tell you whether you wanted to continue. But there are new medical schools opening up here in the United States. The new State of Maine government is going to charter a series of medical lectures at Bowdoin next year. If you were interested in doctoring, you could apprentice with me, study with Reverend Packard as your friend Paul does, and plan to attend Bowdoin in a few years to earn a medical certificate."

Will shook his head. "That sounds like a lot of work."

"You would not have to do everything at once."

"I have never thought about being a doctor." Will hesitated. "Would it matter that I have only one leg?"

"Not for most doctoring. There might be a few patients whose homes you would have trouble getting to, or a few bones you might have trouble setting. But I think you could do it. If you had the interest. It takes caring about people and curiosity about what makes them sick and the strong wish to make them better. Sometimes you can save people's lives."

"As you saved mine."

"Exactly." The doctor sighed. "Of course, at other

times, no matter what a doctor tries, nothing seems to make a difference."

Will thought of Mrs. Theobold lying in the next room.

"If you are interested, perhaps one day you could come with me to see my patients. See what I do."

Will grinned. "I would like that, sir. I would like that fine." Doctoring sounded more interesting than making watches or working in a store. Maybe Dr. Theobold was right. Maybe he had a surgeon's hands. But he needed to find out about other possibilities before he made a commitment that would change his life.

As he walked toward home, Will began to whistle. For the first time in many months he thought about where he was going, instead of how he would get there.

"Dr. Theobold must have given you some good news, Will," said Cassie as they neared Middle Street. "You seem happy."

"Perhaps," agreed Will. "He has certainly given me ideas to think about."

CHAPTER 21

July 11

Today I woke before the others and, remembering the blueberries that would be ripening in the fields at home, felt restless. After leaving a note so Alice would not worry, I spent the early morning in the mists and dew north of town, hunting for berries. In another week or two there should be many, but I was able to return with sufficient fruit to make the season's first blueberry cakes for us and for the Theobolds. It was a small gesture, but I felt I had done something of importance, as both households enjoyed the tartness of the small berries served with heated honey for sweetness. Mrs. Theobold seemed especially grateful and was able to eat several bites. I do not mind doing chores when their result makes life better for others. If what I do can make a difference, can improve someone else's life, if only for a moment, then it is worth doing.

Will woke to find Cassie had already risen. For a moment he thought he had slept long, but the low shadows on the wall told him the day was still new. He stretched and made a decision in the quiet of the room. This would be the day his courage would be strong enough. He looked carefully at the carvings he had left beside his bed in anticipation, and selected two: a strong standing moose, which he felt was one of his best, and the carving of Alice's head, which Dr. Theobold and Mr. Dann had praised, and which he had been perfecting against this day. He dressed quickly, put the two figures in his pocket, and went downstairs.

"Cassie must have woken before the dawn," Alice said as she kneaded the day's wheat bread. "There's beef pie for your breakfast on the hearth. Aaron left early for the store this morning. A brig from Boston came in yesterday carrying many crates that needed unloading."

"Where is Cassie?" Will reached down and took the pie with him back to the table.

"Blueberrying," she said. "I suspect it's early for berries, but perhaps she needed to walk alone for a time. Some days she's more restless than you, Will. I remember when she was little, she would rather be playing outside, even in wintertime, than practicing her stitches by the hearth."

Will grinned. "Cassie can sew a straight line, but she's not one for spending hours at the task, that's for certain. She had better find a patient man for a husband."

"And what have you planned for the day?"

"I will do some walking." Will felt the carvings in his pocket and hoped he would not lose his nerve. "Dr. Theobold told me to keep moving, to get my body used to the leg and teach it how to walk with a smoother gait."

Alice covered the yellow bowl full of dough and put it near the window, where the sun would aid its rising. "If you find yourself near John Stacy's store later this morning, I'd appreciate your stopping in to tell Aaron I could use some salt and another skein of that dark blue silk embroidery floss I'm using in my quilt patches. If he could bring them home tonight, it would be a help."

"I'll tell him," promised Will. "But you don't have to wait for the end of the day. I will bring them home to you."

"I would appreciate that. Now, I need to press two of Aaron's shirts before the heat of the day." Alice put two heavy sadirons and one box iron on the hearth close to the fire to heat them. "I fear this day will be a scorcher. A day to get difficult work done early. Don't tire yourself in the sun, Will."

"I promise to rest when I need to." Will finished his pie. "I plan to walk down by the wharves, where there might be a river breeze."

Alice nodded and turned to pump water to dampen the wrinkled shirts.

The day was a clear one, and the wharves were

already loud with the sounds of seamen's voices intermingled with the creaking of ropes, the crashes of crates lifted into or off of vessels, and the squeaking of wheels as horses pulled wagons full of maritime supplies and cargoes up and down Water Street and onto one of the thirteen wharves that bordered Wiscasset to the east.

Will had already noted the building where Captain Morgan's office was located.

This warm day the door to the office stood open. Will hesitated a moment before entering. Was he bold enough to ask? And the asking could be just the first step.

He stepped carefully over the threshold. A young man not many years older than Will, but much more formally dressed, sat at a large pine desk near the door. "May I help you?" he asked, looking Will up and down.

"I'd like to speak with Captain Morgan, please," said Will firmly. "I have some business with him."

"The captain is over at Tinkham's this morning, seeing about his new vessel. You might find him there. Or you could stop back this afternoon."

By afternoon he might have lost his courage. "I will seek him at the shipyard. Thank you."

Will continued down Water Street, forcing himself to stay calm. Tinkham's Shipyard was near the end of the street, past three salt stores and around the bend. Dozens of men filled the yard, climbing over scaffolds and ramps, and carrying lumber toward one of three partially finished vessels. The sounds of hammers and saws and the ring of men's voices filled the air.

"Boy, can I help you?" Will looked up to see a tall man standing near him. "Don't be getting too close to the site. Shipyards can be dangerous places. Just last week Josiah dropped a hammer from the deck of Captain Morgan's vessel, and it narrowly missed Silas Chase. Could have made a fair hole in his skull."

"I am looking for Captain Morgan."

"Then, you had best be looking over there." The man pointed to a small building on the west side of the yard. "Last I saw him, he was selecting brass fittings for his newest vessel. Did not look too happy about those offered, either. Captain Morgan is a hard man to please."

Will nodded. "Thank you, sir." He walked toward the building, his steps less confident than before. Perhaps this was not the moment to approach Captain Morgan. Asking him at all was brazen. Coming to the shipyard was even more so. Perhaps he should wait, and meet the captain in his office at some later date.

"Hey, Captain Morgan! This young man says he is here to see you!"

The voice came from behind him as Will saw Captain Morgan emerge from the shed. He had no choice now.

The captain watched him approach. "You're looking for me, boy?"

"Yes, sir."

"About what? Do I know you?"

"I am Will Ames. We met seven weeks ago at Mr. Dann's cabinetmaking shop."

The captain hesitated a moment. "Indeed. I do remember. You were having some custom work done."

"Mr. Dann made me a new leg."

"Which seems to be working well. I hope the work he does for me will do as well. So, how can I help you, Will Ames?"

Will paused a moment and then just said it right out. "Captain Morgan, your new vessel will be needing a figurehead. I would like to carve it for you."

Captain Morgan looked more amused than interested. "And have you carved many figureheads?"

"No, sir. Yours would be the first. But I believe I can do it."

"What makes you think so?"

Will reached into his pocket and took out two carvings. "I can carve, sir. I just have never carved anything the size of a figurehead. But during the past month I have been studying those on the vessels in the harbor and think I could do as well as many. Perhaps better."

The captain looked carefully at the carvings. "You can indeed carve. That is clear. The moose is well crafted, but far from the skill a figurehead would demand." He handed the moose back to Will. "But this face . . . it has the look of a figurehead."

"I could do it. I'm sure I could."

"Carving a figurehead is a very special skill. I know no one in Maine who would attempt it. Figureheads on Maine vessels are carved by men in major cities. Some vessels sail with figureheads carved as far away as England or Spain."

Will stepped backward so he was not standing in the captain's shadow. The sun on his face gave him courage. "I know it would not be easy. But I would like to try."

"How old are you, boy?"

"Thirteen, sir."

"Well, you have more than your share of gumption." Captain Morgan ran his fingers over the small carving. "And you have skill. But whether skill on a carving this small could be translated to a ten-foot figurehead, I do not know."

Will stood, hoping.

"What I had in mind for a figurehead, you understand, is a representation of my daughter, Emily. Do you know Emily?"

"I have seen her in church."

"No doubt. She's a pious young woman, and very special to me, especially since her mother died. I would like a figurehead to show her face, as you have done with this carving, and her hair, long, as though the wind were blowing it back onto the ship's hull." The captain looked at him closely. "I would like to find someone in Maine to carve her face. Someone who could see her and know her beauty."

"Yes, sir."

"But carving a figurehead is an important responsibility. A figurehead incorporates the spirit of a ship. One with the wrong spirit could call up foul winds and bad luck. For me to take a chance on work done by an inexperienced boy could endanger the entire vessel and its crew."

"Captain Morgan, I want to carve your figurehead for you. I love to carve, and I think I could find your Emily in the wood."

"I like your spirit, Will Ames," said Captain Morgan finally. "I have a proposition for you. You carve another figure like this one," he said, handing the carving of Alice back to Will. "Make it larger. Not as big as a figurehead, but size enough to prove you can handle work on a larger scale. Perhaps—three feet high?"

Will nodded.

"Bring the carving to me before summer's end. If I think you have the skill to carve the figurehead, I will give you the commission. The *Wiscasset* will not be ready to sail until spring, so you would have the winter to work on the figure. And Emily would be here to be your model."

"Thank you, sir! Thank you, Captain!" Will grabbed the captain's hand and shook it hard. "I will do a good job for you! I promise!"

"I have not yet given you the commission," cautioned the captain. "But I will not commission anyone else to do a figurehead until the end of September. By then, if your large carving does not indicate as much skill as this smaller one, I will write to Boston to order one from a carver I know there. But I would like this vessel to be one truly from the State of Maine. And I would like to see Wiscasset boasting its own sculptor."

"Yes, sir!"

"Do your best, then, and see me again in two months, Will Ames."

Chapter 22

July 12

I have completed three patches for my rose quilt, each patch a different-shaded blossom, and several embroidered leaves. Alice continues to work her statehood quilt. It has been recently resolved that the State of Maine seal is to picture both a farmer and a seaman, as well as a pine tree, a moose, and the North Star, as Maine is the northernmost state of the Union. Alice is carefully working that difficult design. I am not as patient as she is; the needle slips through my fingers in this summer heat, and my mind travels far from my work. Yesterday I walked down to the river to find a sea breeze, but all I found was the smell of cod being brought in on Union Wharf. I saw Will on Water Street. He was not with Paul, as I had thought, but was conversing with a large, distinguished gentleman with a full beard whom I did not recognize. I believe Will is thinking about Dr. Theobold's idea that he could be a doctor. I wish I could have Will's choices. Even though he has but one leg, men speak with him seriously about his future. Alice says my quilt will be much admired, and that pleases me, to be sure. But when I was helping Will, I felt useful and important. The only times I feel my help is valued now is when I am with Mrs. Theobold. I am learning from her, and from the doctor, how best to care for someone who is ill. Someday such skills may be useful even in my own family, as Will's accident has shown.

The door to Mr. Dann's store and workshop was open to let in the cooling river breezes, but Will could still smell the pungent woods and varnishes.

"Mr. Dann?" As Will called out, the man came through a back door.

"Will! I'm glad you stopped in. How is your leg?"

"You did a fine job, sir. It does not yet feel fully a part of me, but Dr. Theobold says that will take months. I still use my crutch, but I'm able to put more weight on the new leg all the time."

"Splendid!"

Will hesitated. Would Mr. Dann think he was too forward or too impetuous? "I came to see . . . if you wouldn't mind, I have been thinking of Captain Morgan's vessel."

"I would be happy to show you what I'm doing," said Mr. Dann, smiling. "I have only just started on the captain's quarters. It took time for the captain and me to agree on a design. This room"—he pointed to a drawing of an elegantly paneled office—"will be in cherry, and luckily I had some seasoned cherry in stock. The rest of the wood has to be ordered, since the captain wants the other room to be of mahogany."

"Where does mahogany come from?"

"South America. But Captain Morgan has heard of a cabinetmaker in Boston who has some and will sell it for the right price. We will take the coaster down next week to inspect it. If the quality suits, then we will not have to wait months for a vessel from the south to arrive."

"Just obtaining the right wood takes more time than I realized."

"Cabinetmaking is not a profession for someone who is impatient." Mr. Dann looked at Will. "But I suspect you know that already, from your carving."

"And I know that if your knife slips, you can ruin a piece of wood you value highly."

"Your carving is strong, Will. You have a good feel for wood."

"When I was here before, with Dr. Theobold, I heard Captain Morgan mention his need for a figurehead."

"He did."

"I took the liberty of finding him and showing him some carvings I have done. I thought perhaps I could carve a figurehead."

"And what did he say?"

"He said I was young, but that I had skill. He has not yet commissioned a figurehead but would like to find someone in Maine who could carve one." Will took a deep breath. "He said if I did a larger carving, he would look at it and decide then whether he would take a chance on me. So I came here. Mr. Dann, I like to carve more than anything else I can do. I think I could do the figure. But I need advice. And"—Will looked at him earnestly—"the right wood."

"Sit down, Will," said Mr. Dann. "Captain Morgan has given you a great opportunity." He sat down at his desk. "But you must be realistic. You are young. Those who carve figureheads have a great deal of experience. You do have the advantage of being here when Captain Morgan is looking for local men to work on his ship. But even if you do your best work, it may not be what he is thinking of."

"I know that, sir. He said the vessel is to be called the *Wiscasset* and that he would like its figurehead to look like his daughter, Emily."

"Do you know Emily?"

"I have seen her from a distance, at church. She has a strong forehead, and her eyes are set wide. Her nose is a little small. I need to observe her more closely."

Mr. Dann smiled. "You have a good eye."

"The captain liked my carving of Alice. He liked

the way her hair fell, long. He said he would like his daughter to look like that on the figurehead."

"And you want to try."

"Very much. I plan to try the larger carving. Will you help me?"

"I will help you to find a suitable piece of pine—I may even have one in my shop that would do—and I will be happy to advise you in any way I can. But Will, I am not a wood carver. The design and the carving would have to be your own."

"They will be, sir." Will grinned. He had not felt this much excitement in many months. "This is what I want to do. But . . ." He hesitated. "Succeeding in such a project will be difficult. I do not want my family and friends to watch me fail. For now I will tell them only that I am doing a larger carving of Alice, as a gift for her and Aaron."

"Your secret is safe with me. Now, let us go and look for the right piece of pine for you."

Will shook his hand. "Thank you, Mr. Dann. Thank you!"

"I will enjoy watching you work," said the older man. "And if carving figureheads proves too big a challenge now, perhaps you might help me with my work for Captain Morgan."

"Help you?" Will looked at him incredulously. "Your work is so fine!"

"It is short of perfection, Will. But you are one of

only a few in Wiscasset who will see that, once you learn more. I would be happy to teach you what I know. And I could use your assistance. This is a major project."

"I would be honored to help you, sir."

Just a short time ago he had no idea of what work he might do. Now there were three possibilities in front of him: carving, woodworking, and doctoring.

"Carving the figurehead is by far the most exciting possibility," Will said to himself as he walked home, trying hard to hide his excitement so Alice and Cassie would not notice. "But it is only fair that I consider Dr. Theobold's offer. And working with Mr. Dann would be almost as good as carving. . . ." Perhaps he could not be a farmer; but he had not dreamed that the skill with a knife he had always taken for granted would bring him so many opportunities.

CHAPTER 23

August 4

Mrs. Theobold seems weaker each day. She is a patient woman and rarely complains, even though I know her coughing is painful. The doctor bleeds her every day now. She likes to have Fred and Anne near her, but I try to have them play quietly. When I am not busy with Mrs. Theobold or the children or the kitchen, the doctor has shown me how to grind herbs he has gathered or bought from The Sign of the Mortar down on Fore Street. It seems magical that some plants I thought were merely weeds in the fields can save someone's life if their secrets are known. God has provided cures for illnesses, if we are wise enough to find them. Sometimes I ask many questions, but Dr. Theobold does not seem to mind answering them. Perhaps it takes his thoughts away from his poor wife's health.

"Come along! Sam will be waiting for us!" Paul called upstairs to Will while Alice covered her ears in dismay.

"Boys! Paul, you may just go up and get him."

"I am coming." Will appeared at the top of the stairs. Despite his hurry, he had to descend one step at a time, swinging his wooden leg down and then bending his good leg to join it. "Did you bring anything to eat?"

"I have some dried beef and some raisin scones my mum made."

"Sounds good. Alice?"

Alice shook her head. "Take the rest of the blackberry pie from breakfast. There is cheese in the larder. And cider."

"Grand!" said Paul, grinning.

Will added the food Alice suggested to the basket Paul carried. "We're off! Alice, we'll be home by dark."

"I would think so!" Alice waved them out the door.

It was a hot August Saturday. All week the boys had been planning to go swimming. Will had even decided to take an afternoon off from carving the piece of pine Mr. Dann had found for him, although he hadn't yet decided whether he would actually go into the river. He wasn't worried about the swimming. He was concerned about having to take his harness and leg off in front of the other boys. People were now used to seeing the light-haired boy with the friendly smile and the odd gait around town, but he wasn't sure they would be as comfortable seeing his body unclothed. Or whether *he* would be comfortable with their stares.

The sun felt warm on their shoulders as Paul and Will crossed Main Street and headed toward the inlet. Tinkham's Shipyard was there, and a mill. The customhouse was nearby, and opposite the sail loft were several shops where you could buy salt for preserving meat and fish.

They passed a group of mariners not much older than they were.

"Looks like a couple of fish set to go swimming," called out one of the mariners.

"I wonder why they don't join us," Will said to Paul. "It's a hot day, and they don't appear too occupied at the moment."

"Most mariners don't know how to swim," said Paul. "They think it would be bad luck to learn."

"They risk their lives on deep waters every day they're at sea. Why wouldn't they ensure they could swim?"

Paul shrugged. "Superstition. I heard it from sailors on the passage last year. They believe it is tempting fate to let the waters think you can master them. And to be practical, if they fell overboard into cold waters, they would rather drown quickly than struggle while trying to swim."

"I am glad not to be a mariner, then, on such a hot day," said Will. "Although I have not yet decided whether I am going to swim. At least I'll take my shirt off and dip my foot in the cool water. That will be worth the walk."

"Not even to think of the good food we have," Paul added.

Sam waved to them from the far side of Fore Street. The tide was only an hour or two on the turn, so the water was still low; not yet deep enough to swim in, but plenty deep enough to splash. Several younger boys were already doing just that.

Will, Paul, and Sam settled themselves on a high pile of rocks and driftwood above the water and focused on eating blackberry pie and scones. The food, held in fingers and eaten outside in salt air, tasted twice as good as it would have at home. Overhead three herring gulls chased a crow away from a wharf where a fisherman was unloading his boat near two eider ducks.

It seemed a perfect afternoon.

CHAPTER 24

August 5

Will and his friends are still down at the harbor, and I have a moment to write of today's events, which were truly memorable! Dr. Theobold has told me that if patients come to see him when he is not to home, they are to be sent away and advised of his anticipated return. But today when Mrs. Swallow arrived in such distress, I did not have the heart to turn her away. Mrs. Swallow, who is considerably larger than her name might imply, sobbed in embarrassment that when she was using her best china chamber pot, it suddenly shattered, leaving her sitting on the floor amid slivers of crockery. Because of the delicate position of the pieces of china lodged in Mrs. Swallow, she was in much pain. Mrs. Theobold and the children were napping, to my relief. I helped Mrs. Swallow lie on her stomach and, with the assistance of some nippers I found among the doctor's tools, was able to remove most of the china

before the doctor returned. He then took over the task
and bathed her posterior with soothing willow water.
Dr. Theobold praised my work and agreed I had done
what was right. I cannot help smiling as I remember
Mrs. Swallow's relief and Dr. Theobold's words.

As the afternoon wore on and the tide came in closer, more boys gathered on the rocks and on the skeleton of the old vessel on the mudflats. By late afternoon perhaps twenty boys were splashing in and out of the water, devouring any food they had been able to beg from home and drying off in the warm sun. The sea breeze had come late, but the air was beginning to cool down. Soon they would all head to home in time for Saturday supper, which for most would be the traditional spicy beans that had been baking all day in homes across Wiscasset.

Will stretched in the warm sun. He had removed his shirt but was the only boy whose trousers were still on. The water was tempting, but he had decided the mudflat would be difficult to negotiate with one leg. He knew he would be sorry later tonight for even removing his shirt; he could already feel the burn of the sun on his light skin. He had not often been outside without his shirt this summer, as he would have been in the fields at home. His nose, too, would be dark red by morning.

Paul pulled himself out of the water and shook his

wet hair in Will's direction. "Sure you don't want to come in?" he asked, dropping down next to Will. "The water is wonderfully cool after the sun. Sam and I could help if you had trouble."

"If we were swimming in a creek with a rocky bottom where I could climb out on the sides, then I would be tempted to try. But I do not think I could manage the mud."

Paul nodded. "The mud is a challenge, even with two good legs." He stuck his feet out in demonstration. "Lovely gooey black mud. And I've cut myself several times on razor clams or oyster shells or barnacles. Mum is going to have a fit if I do not soak these feet well before I get home."

"I am heading back soon," said Will. "The breeze is picking up, and I have more work to do on a cart I promised I'd make Fred Theobold for one of his wooden horses. Cassie and I are going to stop in to see the Theobolds after church tomorrow."

Sam pulled himself out of the water and joined them. "Guess who just arrived?"

Paul and Will looked over to Fore Street. Davey and Thom Pendleton were already removing their shirts and preparing to wade in.

Paul shook his head. "Our favorite friends. Will and I were just thinking about heading to home, in any case. I am not in a mood to cope with those bullies."

Sam stood up. "I would not want them to think we

were leaving because of them. They do not run this town."

"Maybe not," said Will, "but they do get in the way of people living their own lives."

Paul nodded. "That is the truth."

As they watched, Davey and Thom splashed water at a little boy who had been wading near the shore. The boy fell down twice before managing to get himself out of the water and mud. He ran away down Fore Street crying.

"It's not right," Sam said. "Someone should stop them."

The Pendleton brothers got out of the water and headed toward the *United States,* which stretched across the mud to the shore and was used by the older boys as a diving platform. Getting to the higher sections of the ship meant passing near to where Will and his friends sat.

"Well, look who we have here! The crip and his two protectors." Davey looked down at Will. "Looks like someone was not brave enough to go for a little swim today."

"Afternoon, Davey. It's been peaceful here without you two," Sam said.

"Sounds boring to me," Thom answered.

"Water's good today," Paul added. "Enjoy your swim."

"I think we would really like some company, wouldn't we?"

"Swimming with just the two of us is no fun," agreed Davey.

Perhaps it was a coincidence, but most of the boys who had been swimming only moments ago had climbed out and were pulling their shirts on and heading back for the streets of town.

"We would not want to swim alone. You fellows will swim with us, right?"

"Usually we would be honored to do that, of course," said Paul. "But as it happens, we were just talking of returning home. Previous engagements, you know."

Will couldn't help grinning. Paul's English phrasing seemed even more out of context than usual on a mudflat in Wiscasset.

Paul got up and pulled his dry shirt over his head. "Perhaps on another occasion."

"I think we would prefer your company today," said Davey. He stepped close to Paul. "Perhaps just one short swim before you keep your highfalutin 'engagement'?"

"No, thank you," added Sam. "Paul told you we were about to go." He reached down to help Will up. The rocks were not easy to negotiate.

"Look!" Davey said suddenly. "There is one of Will's cousins, out there on the mudflat." Surprised, all three boys turned to see what he was pointing at.

A great blue heron had been walking slowly through

the shallow waters, hunting for minnows, and had now struck a pose on one leg as he quietly waited out his prey.

"Well, Heron Boy, what do you think?" Thom moved closer to Will. "Your one-legged cousin over there seems to like the water. Why don't you join him?"

Anger contorted Will's face. Suddenly Davey stepped toward him and pushed him, hard. It caught Will off balance, and he fell backward into the water. Sam punched Davey from the side. In a few moments they were all in the muddy river.

Will gasped and tried to stand upright. The water wasn't over his head, but he couldn't balance. His wooden leg wanted to float, but it was tied to him by his heavy boot and the leather harness around his waist. It was a struggle to keep his head above the water. He tried to remain calm. But his legs were opposing each other. He couldn't get both down so he could walk on them, and the heavy waters were pulling him under. Finally he tried to lie in the water, floating, holding both legs up, and slowly pulled himself toward the shore. At least that way he could breathe.

He heard struggling and splashing as the other boys fought, but he concentrated on getting himself out of the water. Every part of his body focused on the rocks and driftwood near the shore. He had to get there.

The salt of the tidal river stung his throat and his eyes and made him choke. Finally he reached out and grabbed a large rock on the shore and was able to pull himself up. As he did so, he saw Paul, to his left, also getting out of the water. He looked around. Sam was swimming to shore close by. Davey and Thom were in the water laughing.

"See, Heron Boy? The water is just the right place for you!" Will could see blood pouring from Davey's nose as he trod water. Paul and Sam had done what they could. Both of them reached Will at the same time.

Without saying anything, they each took one of Will's arms and half carried him over the rocks and up to the road. "I could have made it," Will protested. But part of him was glad for the help. Dry and calm he probably could have made his own way over the rocks. Wet and furious, with the leather strapping rubbing him in places he didn't even want to think of, the help was welcome.

None of the boys said anything more until they had walked several blocks.

Then Will said, "We have to show them."

Paul and Sam nodded. "Yes."

"I have an idea." The other boys looked at Will. "Let me think it out. You are with me, right?"

"We're with you," Sam promised.

"All the way," agreed Paul as they each headed home.

Will smiled to himself. It just might work. And if it did, it would make the Pendleton brothers look foolish. He just had to plan carefully. He was whistling to himself before he got to the steps of his house.

CHAPTER 25

August 5, Late Evening

Boys can be very foolish! Will returned home this evening soaking wet after an afternoon with Paul and Sam. He had gone swimming in his leg and harness! He removed them as soon as he was home, of course, and I rinsed the leather in fresh water to remove the salt. Then we both tried to stretch out the strapping and left it to dry in the little sun that was left tonight. Despite our efforts, I fear it will shrink. And after two months of softening the leather and ensuring it fit properly! I scolded Will, but his mind seemed filled by other thoughts. His leg is now propped up near the stove. He has finished a toy he was whittling for Fred and is now reading a book and seems unconcerned. Boys have no sense at all!

Will had to miss church. His leg and harness were still damp, and despite his pulling them, he was afraid Cassie was right: The leather straps had shrunk. They might all need to be replaced. And until that was done, Will would be back to using his crutch alone.

He sat in the backyard, and his chisel made deep inroads into the thick, forty-inch piece of pine. He had told Alice the carving was for her, and no one had questioned him. They were used to Will's whittling. But this piece was by far the largest and most difficult project he had ever undertaken.

It was too massive for the delicate work he usually did. He moved back to see what details showed up from a distance. Alice's face looked down, as though she were rocking a baby, and long strands of her hair made a sort of wreath around the face. It didn't look yet as much like Alice as he had hoped, and he knew she would have preferred to be carved with her hair secured on the top of her head, as a woman's should be, but Captain Morgan had liked the earlier carving, and Will had decided to concentrate on the flow of the hair, as well as details in the face. He wanted to capture the private moments when Alice would be alone with her baby.

Will's mind raced between the carving and the captain's decision about it that could determine his future, and his resolve to make fools of Davey and Thom Pendleton. Any plans for that would have to wait until he could use his leg again. And until he had done some more planning.

The front door closed and Cassie called out, "Will! Will? Where are you?"

"I am out back." He was sitting in the shade. His nose and back were sore from yesterday's sun.

Cassie joined him.

"How was church? Did you give the cart to Fred? At least I managed to finish that last night."

Cassie was silent.

Will looked at her closely. "Are you all right? What has happened?"

"So much, Will. I cannot think of it all at one time." She sat on the granite step and took off her bonnet.

"Then, just tell me one thought at a time."

"Before church boys were racing about outside, as they often do before services begin."

Will nodded.

"I heard them talking. Davey Pendleton pushed you into the river yesterday, didn't he? You did not go swimming of your own volition, as you told me."

Will sighed. "He pushed me. But I was all right, Cassie. I got myself out."

She reached over and looked at his palm. "How did you get those cuts and scratches?"

"I got out of the water by pulling myself up onto the rocks. I was cut by barnacles. That's all." Will took his hand back and kept carving. "It's nothing. My hands don't hurt."

"They called you Heron Boy at church."

Will put his knife down. "And?"

"And I hate it! It isn't fair! How can they be so mean!"

"Were all the boys saying that?"

"No. Just Davey and Thom. But others were listening."

"Don't worry, Cassie. I have a plan. Soon people will be laughing at them, not at me."

"What are you going to do?"

"I can't tell you yet. But you can help if you would like to."

"I would! I would like to very much."

"Did you stop at the Theobolds'?"

"No. I was too upset; I wanted to talk with you, so I came right home. Alice and Aaron were going to stop there. Dr. Theobold and the children weren't in church."

"Why don't you go there now. I'm fine. And I promised Fred that cart. You can take it to him."

Cassie nodded. "I will. And don't forget, Will. Whatever your plan is for the Pendleton boys, I want to be part of it."

"You'll be there, Cassie. I promise."

CHAPTER 26

The next time the door closed, Will knew it was not Cassie. The footsteps were too heavy, and no one called out to him. *It must be Alice and Aaron,* he thought. He was getting hungry; he was glad Alice had returned to start dinner.

He tucked his knives and chisels into a small cloth bag. Since he was again using the crutch, it was much easier to carry things in a bag he could hang on his wrist or shoulder than it was to depend on his hands.

Aaron came out to him. "Will?" Aaron walked into the sunshine and sat on a rock that had been too big to move. It now made a seat near Alice's tomato plants. "I have some sad news."

Will looked at him. If Aaron were going to tell him about the boys at church, that would have made him angry, perhaps, or inspired his pity. But anger and pity were not the expressions on Aaron's face.

"Mrs. Theobold died last night."

Will felt as though the ground were suddenly less solid under his foot. "I know she has been ill."

Aaron nodded. "For a long time. The doctor was able to make her more comfortable, but there are many illnesses God has given us that cannot be cured."

"Where is Cassie?"

"At their house. Alice and some other women from the church are going to help lay Mrs. Theobold out, and Cassie is staying with Fred and Anne."

Will nodded. To lose their mother must be very hard. They were so young. He and Cassie were lucky Ma was well. What would Fred and Anne do without a mother?

"There are going to be services tomorrow," Aaron went on. "We will all attend, of course."

"I may need help getting up the hill across the Green to the church."

"You will have whatever help you need."

"Dr. Theobold saved my life, but he wasn't able to save his wife's." How must that make him feel? Will wondered how the doctor could find the courage to continue practicing medicine after being unable to save someone he loved.

"The doctor is grieving deeply. She was almost thirty; they had been married ten years."

"How can God let that happen?" Will blurted out. "How can He let me live, without even a leg to walk on, and let a wife and mother die? It isn't fair!"

"It does not seem fair," Aaron agreed. "But it must be part of His plan. If there were no plan, then life would be chaos. There would be no purpose and no direction."

"Well, I wish He would tell us what His plan is," Will added. "Because it makes no sense to me. No sense at all." He put his head down on his arms so he couldn't see the sunshine. It wasn't right that the sun shone brightly on such a day.

CHAPTER 27

September 5

*It is just over a year since Will's accident. In Woolwich,
Pa and the boys must be haying and threshing the
wheat. That all seems very far from here. In recent
weeks I have spent much of my time at the Theobold
home. Mrs. Theobold is buried in the old cemetery not
far from the family and house she loved. The doctor and
Fred and Anne visit her grave almost every day and have
planted roses there. She loved her roses so much. The
doctor is despondent, and Anne and Fred need someone
to watch out for them and do their washing and keep the
house in order. Many women in Wiscasset brought food
in the first weeks after Mrs. Theobold's death, but they
do so less often now. I have tried to cook enough to
ensure the family is not concerned over food. I am also
grinding some of the doctor's medicines, under his
direction. I am learning all I can. A small difference in
a dosage of medicine can make a very large difference to*

a patient. Yesterday I helped still the arm of a young boy whose shoulder had become dislocated, while the doctor put the bone back into place. But most days I stay with Fred and Anne, much as I find Dr. Theobold's work of more interest than I do his kitchen. Will spent much of August occupied at home, working at his carving of Alice. But his new harness and braces are now comfortable for him to wear for several hours, and soon he will be able to spend time with the doctor, to see if he would want a future in medicine. What a wonderful future that would be! If I were a boy, I would be very thankful for such an opportunity. But Will seems to care more about his whittling.

Will and Cassie walked through the soft mists of the early-autumn morning up the road to the Theobolds' house. "On Thursdays the doctor visits the jail," Cassie advised Will. "And then he drives up the Alna Road a piece and checks on several families there."

"It is a beautiful day for a drive." Will took a deep breath. The elm and maple leaves were only just beginning to turn. The last of the goldenrod was drying in the corners of yards, as were the tall milkweed stalks, which only two weeks ago had been covered by orange and brown butterflies.

Between finishing his carving of Alice and planning a way to get back at the Pendleton brothers, Will had not noticed until now: Summer was over.

"I will pack some food for you and the doctor, in case your visits take you past dinner hour," Cassie said, thinking out loud. "But you will certainly be home by supper. And I'll take Fred to school this morning, and then Anne and I can perhaps trim some of Mrs. Theobold's roses. They need to be pruned and tied up before the frost and snows come."

Will laughed. "Cassie, you sound like a little mother. Dr. Theobold can take care of those things."

"A doctor is an important person who must think of the needs of others," Cassie responded tartly. "Dr. Theobold does not have time for household details. Those are women's tasks."

"I see," said Will with a grin.

"Remember all that you do and see today, Will, so you can tell me tonight! You are so lucky that the doctor is taking an interest in you!"

"You are right," agreed Will. "And I'm sure there is a lot I don't know about doctoring."

The Theobold children were dressed and in the kitchen when Cassie and Will arrived, although Cassie checked to see that Fred's hair was combed and Anne's apron tied properly. The doctor seemed relieved that she was there to tend to such details, and he went to get his box of medical tools and medicines.

"You can ride on the wagon seat with me, Will," he said as he put the box in the back of his wagon. "Now that you're doing so well with your leg, you can brace yourself with it."

Will agreed, and the doctor helped him up to the high seat.

"Our first stop is the jail," the doctor explained. "I visit the inmates there once a week, unless the jailer sends for me betweentimes."

"Are those in jail so sick?"

"Often. But the number of people in the jail varies greatly. In recent times only a few people have been there for having committed crimes. The others are debtors or those whose minds are confused. There are also spaces for those with contagious illnesses and for any women or children who are confined."

"Children? In jail?"

"Some are the children of women who are imprisoned for various crimes. And occasionally a child is imprisoned on his own behalf. Last year a boy about your age was sentenced to several months in the jail for stealing apples."

By the time Will could think about that, Dr. Theobold had stopped his horse in front of a three-story granite building. At the base of the building the stones were more than three feet thick, and they were only slightly narrower on the higher stories. "Is there heat in the winter?" Will asked as the doctor helped him down from the wagon seat.

"There is a woodstove in the hallway outside each floor of cells. Nevertheless, the cells are unheated, and in winter they can be very cold and damp."

Will shivered.

"Who is here now?"

"Only two men, and neither has a contagious disease, or I would have been called since last week." They walked up to the jailer's house, which was attached to the jail. "Until recently all serious criminal cases were taken to Massachusetts to be tried, and those who were judged guilty were imprisoned there. Now that Maine is a state, the Lincoln County Jail may find itself much busier." He rapped on the door. "If you should choose to apprentice with me, checking on the prisoners here would soon become part of your responsibilities."

The heavy wooden door was opened by a tall man with a circle of keys on his belt.

"Good morning! This is Will Ames, who is assisting me today."

The jailer nodded glumly. "Little for you to do today, Doctor. Only the same two you saw last week, and you'll find them unchanged."

"I will just take a look, then." Dr. Theobold pushed the door a little to get in, and Will followed him. The jailer unlocked the chain on a heavy iron door to his right. "Don't be taking too long, now. I have other chores to do than seeing to the comfort of criminals."

"They are men," the doctor replied.

"Men who have gone afoul of the law and are getting as they deserve."

The heavy door swung open into a wood hallway to

the cell area. "Follow me." The jailer walked ahead of them down several steps into the lowest level, where he unlocked still another barred iron door. Beyond it was a passageway, all of granite, including the ceiling and uneven floor. Will walked carefully so as not to slip.

There were three doors on each side of the hall. In each door was a small opening set high in the door.

The jailer opened the first door on the right. "Alcox! The doc is here to see that you are still alive!" A gray-bearded man slowly rose from a pile of dirty blankets on a crude bedstead.

Dr. Theobold went over to him. "Still coughing, Joseph?"

The man coughed deeply, as if to demonstrate. "Can't seem to shake it, Doc. Other summers I've improved some, but this year the sun didn't work a cure."

Will looked around the cell. In addition to the bedstead there was only a stinking wooden barrel used as a chamber pot, a dirty plate, and a small, high window covered by bars. How could sun have reached such a place at all?

The doctor pulled a bottle out of his pocket. "Here is some more red cabbage syrup, Joseph, for your chest. I'm also leaving you some poppy water to help you sleep when the coughing gets too bad. Keep as warm as you can." He looked at the jailer standing in the doorway. "Do you have additional bedding that could be given to this man?"

"He's done well enough with what he has had in the past."

"The season is changing. Some additional blankets would be of help," Dr. Theobold said. "If there is not budget for it, perhaps I could mention the need to Judge Greene when I see him tomorrow?"

"That will not be necessary."

"Joseph, I will visit you next week."

"Thank you, Doc, for seeing to me."

"You are most welcome." The words were almost lost as the thick door closed. "My next patient?"

"There is only the one other this week. And he's a complainer." The jailer opened another cell door. In the dark room beyond was a younger man, perhaps twenty-five, seated on a bedstead similar to Joseph's. He did not get up. Both his wrists and ankles were shackled with heavy iron bands.

"What was the need for shackles?" asked Dr. Theobold as he entered the cell.

Will felt as though he would go mad just seeing this place and smelling it. The air was putrid. This prisoner was not even in a position to use his chamber pot and had soiled his clothing, such as it was.

"The man complains about the food, about the air, about everything," said the jailer. "I told him if he did not shut up, then I would do something to stop his talking. He refused to shut up."

Will watched as the doctor examined the inmate's

wrists and ankles. They were raw and bleeding from the rubbing of the iron cuffs. "Will, get the small blue pail in my wagon now, please," he said. He then turned to the jailer. "This man has learned his lesson for now. For medical reasons I think you might remove the shackles."

The jailer grunted a little but did as the doctor said and took the shackles outside the cell, where he hung them close, ready for use again.

Will came back with the pail, and the doctor rubbed liniment moistened with willow water over the inmate's sores. "This should take down some of the swelling and aid healing," he explained. "Now, Silas," he said to the man on the bed. "This is not an easy life you are living, but the jailer can make it even more difficult for you. It would be best if you'd listen to him." Silas nodded. Dr. Theobold touched the man's shoulder as he left.

The jailer locked the door and closed it with a *thud*.

"Thank you for taking the time," said Dr. Theobold. "The men will appreciate it."

"Not likely."

"And you will remember the extra blankets for Mr. Alcox?"

"All will be in order when you come again next week, Doctor."

"In the meantime, should you need me, you know where I can be found."

"What did those men do?" asked Will as he and Dr.

Theobold got back in the wagon and started up the road out of town. "Why are they in jail? That old man looked so sick!"

"The *old* man? He is about thirty years old but has been in jail for six. He was in a tavern fight and a man was killed. He has consumption and probably won't last the winter. But at least he should be kept warm."

Will shivered. The man had looked fifty years old, not thirty. "And the other man?"

"He stole a horse. Has another year before his sentence is up."

Will was quiet as they headed up the Alna Road. He was not sure this day would convince him to be a doctor. But it had convinced him not to commit a crime.

CHAPTER 28

"What patients did you see, Will? What did the doctor do?" Cassie walked next to him on their way home.

"We visited two men in the jail," Will said. "One had a coughing illness, as Mrs. Theobold did, and one some sores that needed liniment. Then we visited three families in Alna. One man needed a tooth pulled. I helped hold his head while the doctor pulled it out with those iron pliers he has. The man yelled as though he were being murdered, despite the rum he had drunk even before we arrived."

"And the other patients?"

"A woman whose back was covered by running sores. The doctor gave her some lotion for them."

"What kind of lotion?"

"I don't remember. It was sort of yellow looking. And then there was a family with six or seven children; they were all yelling and running about, so I'm not sure how many. Last year one of the boys had an ear infection and no one called a doctor, so the infection wasn't treated; now the boy is deaf. Dr. Theobold said he tries to stop in there every couple of weeks to see if anyone needs doctoring. The children live with their father in a house with little food and much dirt."

"Where is their mother?"

"She died giving birth to the youngest one. The father should be farming and caring for his family, but he spends the little he has on drink. The doctor gave me a long lecture on the evils of alcohol on our trip home, despite his having prescribed it for the man with the rotten tooth."

"What will happen to those children?"

"Dr. Theobold is going to ask Reverend Packard to help find some families in the church to take them in. If not, they will have to go to Mr. Trundy's poorhouse."

Cassie and Will walked in silence for a few minutes.

"Doctoring is more complicated than I thought," Cassie said. "I imagined it would be healing people. And I suppose, in a way, it is. But the situations of most of the people you saw today could not be fixed with just medicine."

"He cured the man with the bad tooth. That was the simplest visit of the day. Although"—Will looked down at his left hand—"it was painful in other ways."

Cassie looked down too. "Will! The man bit you?"

"He didn't mean to, Cassie. He was in so much pain he didn't know what he was doing."

"He should have thanked you, not bitten you!"

Will grinned at her. "It's all right, Cassie. Today I learned that a doctor isn't always thanked for what he does."

CHAPTER 29

September 15

I continue to work with Dr. Theobold, and Will has spent several days with him in the past week. It aggravates me that Will's mind does not seem to be on doctoring, but on the whispered plans he is making with Sam and Paul. He also spent several days doing I know not what down on the wharves and was not available either to the doctor or to Alice. He seems content and smiles to himself often, but I wish he would share his thoughts with me. September is half gone. In early October we return home for Nathan and Martha's wedding, and Pa and Ma expect us to stay. I have talked with Dr. Theobold and with Alice about possibilities for remaining in Wiscasset, but Will makes no plans that I can see. Perhaps he will be able to think more clearly once his plan for the Pendleton brothers has been acted out. As I write this, he and Sam are in the back of the house talking again. Tomorrow is the night for what

Will has planned. The weather has to be fine and the timing right. I have my fingers crossed that all shall happen as he hopes. I intend to be there to see every moment of it!

On a September Saturday afternoon Davey and Thom Pendleton could usually be found standing around the town pump on Main Street. There was no school on Saturdays, and most masters let their apprentices take the afternoon off. It was too chilly now for swimming, but not yet cold enough to have to find an inside location. Often they were joined by other boys, but Davey and Thom would be there for sure.

Will was not usually among those who stood watching wagons filled with pumpkins and squashes and potatoes coming to town, but today he had a reason to be there.

"I want to go too," Cassie begged. "Please, let me come!"

"No," Will answered, pulling her long hair a bit to show he did care about her. "If you were there, Davey and Thom would want to show off. They wouldn't act naturally. But you can come tonight. Alice agreed."

They had talked long about that the night before, but finally Alice had said Cassie might go, as long as Will stayed close by her. Alice was getting larger every day, and as the time for the baby got closer, she was more and more careful about what she did, and

to their distraction, about what Cassie and Will did
too.

"I'll be back soon enough to tell you all that happened." Will left, walking at a good pace. It was finally
going to happen! It had taken careful planning, but this
was the day. Sam was going to meet him at the corner,
and Paul would come along a little later, just in case
there were any problems. But there could be none. His
plan was too perfect.

Davey and Thom and several other boys, including
Sam, were where Will had predicted: on the corner, calling out comments to passing wagons and riders, and
making quiet remarks about any girls or women who
happened to walk nearby.

Will took a deep breath and walked to the corner.
"Afternoon, Davey, Thom, Sam."

"Heron Boy has decided to join us this afternoon."
Davey bowed low before him. "We are indeed honored
by your presence."

"I came because I knew you'd all be here. I need your
help. You have lived in Wiscasset longer than I, so I was
sure you'd be able to tell me the truth."

"We know everything that happens in this town,
don't we, boys!" Davey grew at least an inch or two in
establishing his authority. "What seems to be bothering
you, Heron Boy?"

"You all know my sister and I sometimes help Dr.
Theobold."

The boys nodded. Davey was right about one thing: Everyone in Wiscasset knew what everyone else did.

"It is getting dark earlier in the evening now, and I have to walk near the old graveyard on my way home to Middle Street." Will leaned over and whispered loudly, "I've seen ghosts rising from the graves there!"

"What?" Thom looked at him. "That cemetery has been there forever. It has graves going back to my great-grandfather's time. But I never heard of anyone seeing ghosts. Of course"—he looked directly at Will—"maybe the ghosts just scare people who don't belong in Wiscasset."

Will ignored Thom's comments. "I heard a story of a boy—a boy about your age, Thom—who was killed by the British army during the Revolution. He was shot up so bad they had to bury him in pieces. And somewhere between where he was shot and his grave, they lost one of his hands. So now he rises from his grave at night searching for it."

Davey and Thom looked at each other. "I never heard that story," said Davey. "Any of you boys ever hear that?"

Will and Paul and Sam had done their work well. There were many boys in town who wanted to see Davey and Thom proved foolish. Two of the boys nodded. "I've heard of that ghost," said one boy from in the back of the group.

"I heard about it first thing I came to town," said Sam. "For sure. Mr. Wright told me to stay away from the old cemetery at night because you never knew who—or what—might be there."

"I don't believe it," said Davey. "I am not afraid of any old cemetery."

"Would you go there, then, with me tonight and see?" asked Will hopefully. "I would feel much reassured knowing there is truly no ghost there. It has scared my little sister, Cassie, too. In fact, if you boys would all go with Cassie and me tonight, I would be obliged."

"I'm not sure," said Davey. "I don't believe there are ghosts down in the cemetery, but still, my ma has chores she'll be wanting me to do tonight."

"You wouldn't be scared, would you?" asked Sam. "Scared to go with Heron Boy and his little sister to a place you know there are no ghosts?"

"I'm not scared," said Thom. "Come on, Davey, we can go! We have nothing planned for tonight. And it will not take long to show this Heron Boy and his baby sister there is nothing to be afeared of."

"Then, we can all meet here at midnight tonight?" Will tried to look very innocent.

"Midnight!"

"To make it a good test, we have to give the ghost the best chance to come out. And midnight's the time for ghosts to rise from their graves, right?"

All the boys nodded. That was common knowledge.

"You will be able to sneak out, won't you? After your ma is asleep?"

"We do that all the time," Davey boasted. "Midnight is a good hour."

"Best part of the evening," said Thom.

"Then, it's set. We'll meet here at midnight," Will said. "I'm really glad all of you are so brave, because I walk past that graveyard every night, and thinking of that poor boy looking for his hand has given me nightmares."

"We'll be there," said Davey. "We're not scared like you and your little sister. Maybe your name should be Chicken Boy instead of Heron Boy."

"Till midnight, then," said Will, heading back toward home.

"Midnight!" Thom called after him.

CHAPTER 30

The weather held, and the night was just as Will had planned it: dark, with only a little light from stars and from the new moon. When he and Cassie got to the corner shortly before midnight, Davey and Thom and several other boys were waiting.

Davey paced nervously. "I cannot believe you got half the town out of bed in the middle of the night, Heron Boy," said Davey. "And you even brought your baby sister to take care of you, just as you said."

Will squeezed Cassie's hand hard, warning her to be quiet.

"I appreciate all of you coming out to help me," Will said quietly. "If I know there are no ghosts, then I will feel much better. Especially about walking near that dark cemetery at night."

"Me too," Cassie said, pretending to be very scared.

"Well, we don't want any girls to be scared of

ghosts, now do we?" said Thom, swaggering a bit in front of Cassie.

"Now that we are all here, let's go!" a voice came from the back of the group. "My ma will kill me if I am not awake to do morning chores before church or fall asleep during prayers tomorrow."

"That is a good idea," Will said. "To pray. Ghosts are afraid of prayer, aren't they?"

Davey looked around at the other boys, several of whom were nodding in agreement. "Guess it wouldn't do any harm to pray. Just in case."

Cassie squeezed Will's hand again as her clear voice was heard over the group. "I think we should start toward the cemetery now and pray as we go." Before any of the boys had time to react, she turned and headed toward the cemetery. The boys followed. They wouldn't be outdone by any girl. And as her voice started to say the familiar words, the boys all joined in. "'The Lord is my shepherd; I shall not want. He maketh me to lie down in green pastures . . .'"

It was only a few blocks to the graveyard. As they approached, Will whispered, "Turn down your lanterns! We don't want the ghosts to see us coming."

They walked quietly into the dark graveyard. Near the entrance was a slight mound of earth. Silently Will led them up the little hill. There was no sound except the crunching of fallen leaves under nervous feet. Suddenly, from the far corners of the graveyard, there rose a strange humming, groaning noise. It started low and then it grew. Louder. And louder. And louder still.

Not one boy—or girl—moved.

Will cried out, "Come out, ghosts! Show yourselves! If you are there, prove it to us!"

The other boys moved back as, suddenly, there was a sense of movement in the graveyard. Rounded white shapes rose from the ground.

Davey and Thom screamed and ran as fast as they could. No one else moved.

Then, before the brothers had disappeared, laughter erupted. Cassie's giggling was loud enough to let the boys know something was wrong.

Davey and Thom stopped.

Cassie's voice rose over the laughter. "Those ghosts have tails!"

As Davey and Thom looked back, the white forms in the graveyard moved and appeared to rise from the ground.

Then the moonlight made them clear.

A herd of sheep had been sleeping in the cemetery. When the eerie sounds awakened them, they had slowly gotten to their feet. Sam and Paul came running from the far corners of the burying ground, each carrying the large conch shell they had used as a horn. Conch horns were common enough in a town filled with mariners who had sailed southern waters, but not common in a graveyard at midnight.

All the boys turned and pointed at Davey and Thom, laughing loudly. They all had been in on the trick.

"Guess you were right, Thom. There aren't any ghosts here!" Will said seriously.

The other boys doubled up in laughter as Davey and Thom stood, furious and embarrassed.

As the brothers stomped their way home, the rest of the boys and Paul and Sam and Will clapped one another on the shoulders and grinned. "We still have a long night ahead of us," said Paul. "We have to get all of Mrs. Pickle's sheep back to the Green. But it was worth it to hear Davey and Thom Pendleton scream!"

Three of the sheep bleated in agreement as the boys scattered to the corners of the graveyard and started herding the animals back toward the Green. This night would long be remembered.

CHAPTER 31

October 6

We have been busy making preparations for tomorrow's journey back to Woolwich to see Nathan and Martha wed. Alice's baby is active as her time nears, so I did most of the baking necessary. I have greatly increased my knowledge of cooking these past months. Ma will be pleased at that. We made apple cake and biscuits, and are taking along comfits, two kinds of pickles, and a ham. Alice has finished her State of Maine quilt as a gift to warm Nathan and Martha's wedding bed, and I have made them two quilted pillow covers embroidered with their initials to match the quilt. Aaron is bringing them spices and sugar and tea from Mr. Stacy's store. Will has carved a chickadee, a cardinal, and a song sparrow for them, as Martha loves birds. I can hardly believe Will and I have been away from home more than five months. Last October, Will's future seemed bleak. Now we return to Woolwich not only with wishes

of happiness for Nathan and Martha, but also with
wishes for our own futures. I am anxious to see Ma and
Pa and Ethan and the boys. But I am even more anx-
ious to know their reactions to our plans. I'll not sleep
tonight for the wondering. Will we be returning to
Wiscasset? Or will Ma and Pa decree we are to stay on
the farm?

Saturday dawned crisp and clear. Maple and elm and
sumac leaves colored the ground yellow and orange and
red. It would have been a beautiful day for any activity.
But this day was special because it was Nathan and
Martha's wedding day. Alice, big with her child, climbed
slowly into Aaron's wagon, and Cassie snuggled next to
her under a large quilt. Will sat up front with Aaron.

The wedding was to be at Martha's home, with
family and a few neighbors present. "What dress do you
think she will wear?" Cassie asked. "Martha has three or
four dresses, but she might have made herself a new one."

Alice smiled. "In the months before their wedding
most women spend their time weaving blankets and
patching quilts and preparing linens. But Martha has
always loved clothes. We will have to see." She looked at
her younger sister. "I wonder if the family will recognize you, Cassie. You have grown so over the summer."
They had let out Cassie's two dresses and had made over
one of Alice's for her. Cassie was now nearly as tall as
her sister.

"You're the one who has grown," Cassie threw back. "You're twice as big as when Ma last saw you."

The two sisters laughed together as the wagon, despite Aaron's careful driving, lurched over the rutted road.

They were going home first, and then the family would travel together, with Nathan, to Martha's house. After the ceremony Nathan and Martha would return to the Ames home, where Pa and Nathan and Simon had built a new room onto the house for the newly married couple. That way Ma would have help in the kitchen, Pa would not lose help in the fields, and Nathan would begin establishing his future claim to part of the farm.

Ethan had posted himself as watchman. As soon as the wagon was in sight, he called out, "Ma! Pa! Nathan! Simon! They've come!" And so everyone was there to greet them as they climbed down off the wagon.

Pa stood in the back and smiled proudly as Ma walked over and hugged each one in turn, her eyes filling with tears of joy. "Alice, you look beautiful. You're going to be a wonderful mother to that baby. It seems like yesterday I was carrying you. Will, you look strong and tall with that new leg! We made the right decision about that, without doubt. I am so proud of you. Cassie, you have grown up! Alice has written how much help you have been to her and to poor Dr. Theobold and his children." Ma stood back and looked at them all with pride. "And here Nathan is going off and getting married."

"Ma, I will just be going off for the ceremony and the supper! Martha and I will be right here tonight and tomorrow. And," he added softly and proudly, "forever."

There were more hugs all around as Ethan jumped up and down, running from one of his big brothers or sisters to another. "Will," he said, tugging on Will's new shirt, "Will, I took good care of your animals for you. I did! Come and see!" He pulled Will toward the house.

Alice and Cassie showed Ma the food they had brought. "We'll leave it here in the wagon, since we'll be heading over to the Baileys' soon enough. With all you made, there's no doubt we'll have ample of everything," Ma said. "Now, you all come inside and have some food and drink. We'll have more time to talk now than we will later today, when there will be other events to occupy our minds!"

Pa followed everyone into the house, quieter than Ma but looking just as proud.

They all settled into the kitchen. "This is the way we always sat in the evenings!" Alice said.

Simon teased, "But in the old days you didn't take up quite so much room." Alice blushed and they all laughed.

Cassie sat on the hearth, holding Sunshine, now a full-grown cat, tightly in her arms.

Pa was the first one to bring up the future. "I didn't

notice many bags in that wagon. Alice, I know you and Aaron must get back to Wiscasset tonight. But Will and Cassie? You were to be in Wiscasset only for the summer. Summer's past. Time you were to home for the winter."

After a short silence Will spoke. "Pa, you said there was no place on a farm for a man with one leg. At first I was angry with you for saying that. But now I know you were right. I could do some farmwork, but it would not be easy, and it would put an extra burden on others. In Wiscasset I saw other ways for men to live, and with the two legs I have now, there are other possibilities for me."

"He is such a smart boy," put in Alice. "Why, he has been helping Dr. Theobold. The doctor says Will could be a fine surgeon someday."

Pa looked at Will. "So that's what you want, Will? To be a surgeon?"

"Doctoring would be a fine profession," Ma put in proudly.

Will looked down. "It would be fine. And I have given it a lot of thought. But I don't think the practice of medicine is for me."

"Then, what did you have in mind?" Pa said. "Or were you planning just to stay and eat Alice and Aaron out of house and home?"

"Pa—" Alice tried to add a few words.

"No, Alice, this is not your issue. It is for Will and me to decide."

Ma put her hand over Alice's.

"I've been doing more whittling this summer. Carving things."

"Whittling is a fine amusement," said Pa. "But it is not a way to make a living."

"Will made all those animals. He let me play with them," said Ethan, pointing at the dozens of carvings he had lined up neatly against the far wall. "I took good care of them when he was gone!"

"You did just fine, Ethan," said Ma, opening her arms as he came for a hug. "Let the others talk now."

"I have spoken with Mr. Dann. He's the cabinet-maker who made my leg, Pa, and is a fine craftsman. He said I could work with him and learn furniture making. And I might want to do that. But first I want to try a big carving."

"And what is this thing you are going to be carving? And where will you even get the money for the wood? Will, you are thirteen years old! It is time you took responsibility for your future. Carving is not a future!"

"I *am* taking responsibility, Pa," said Will. "I have thought a lot about my future. I met a man in Wiscasset. Captain Morgan is his name. He owns ships, and he is building another now. In July, I showed him a small carving I did of Alice."

Alice looked down and blushed.

"He said it was just the sort of thing he wanted as a figurehead for his new ship. Only bigger." Will took a deep breath. Everyone was quiet. "Mr. Dann got me some wood and I did another carving of Alice, a bigger one, to show Captain Morgan I could do it." Will looked proudly at everyone. "He liked my work. And he's given me a commission to carve a figurehead for the *Wiscasset*, the vessel being built for him this winter."

They all looked at one another in amazement. This was news!

Pa's voice was gentle but questioning. "What do you know about figureheads, Will? You carved little toys for Ethan and nice birds for your ma, I know. But a figurehead . . . that's a big piece. And it must be right, or it will bring bad luck to the captain and crew. Even a farmer knows that."

"Captain Morgan is willing for me to try. In the past he has ordered figureheads from carvers in Boston and Philadelphia. But this ship is to be called the *Wiscasset* and he wants her to boast a figurehead carved in her home port." Will hesitated. "He knows it will be the first time I have attempted such a thing. But he wants me to do it. Mr. Dann has said I may do the work in his shop, and he will be there to give me advice." He paused again. "If the carving is not good enough, then I will have lost a winter. But it will be a winter when I tested myself to see if I could do something well. Something I chose to do."

Will got up and walked over to his father.

"Pa, before the accident I wanted to be a farmer. I

wanted it more than anything in the world. I wanted it so much I couldn't see anything else. But after my accident I had to look at other things. This is what I've found. It may not be right in the end. But I have to try. To give myself this chance."

Pa nodded. His voice was gruff. "You are becoming a man, Will. I'm right proud of you."

Aaron spoke up. "He's welcome to stay with us. We have enjoyed having Cassie and Will with us. And with the baby coming"—he looked sidewise at Alice—"maybe they could be of help sometimes."

Pa looked at his younger daughter. "Cassie, too?"

"Pa." Cassie's voice was strong. "Dr. Theobold will pay me to care for his house and his children and will teach me about herbs and medicines. If I were a boy, I'd want to be a doctor, just like Dr. Theobold. Really, Pa, I would!"

"A she-doctor! I should say not," Pa harrumphed. "You two are getting your minds confused by town life. Women cannot be doctors. Their brains are not strong enough, and it would certainly be improper for them to see and do the sorts of things doctors must."

"I know, Pa," said Cassie. "But a woman could *help* a doctor. A woman could learn about herbs and medicines and tinctures and potions and how to mix them for patients."

"Sounds like something the Indians did, not something for my daughter to do," Pa answered.

"You're right; the Abenaki had considerable skills with plants and herbs. But so do men from Europe. Dr. Theobold said so."

"Apothecaries, you mean," Pa sputtered. "Fancy name for witches, I suspect."

Ma looked at Cassie and gave her a sign to quiet down.

Cassie sighed. "You've met Dr. Theobold, Pa. He's a good man. A widower with children who needs help. The children like me, and his home is only a few blocks from Alice and Aaron's, so I could be of help to them, too, with the baby coming."

No one said anything for a few moments. Then Pa nodded. "Sounds as though you have both settled your lives. Cassie, sounds like Alice and Dr. Theobold could use your help for now. Maybe more than your ma will be needing you here. But you will be missed in Woolwich. And you know if all does not work out as you hope, you will always have places here."

Cassie went over and hugged Pa, and Will shook his hand as Simon and Nathan came over to congratulate him.

Ma stood up. "It sounds as though it is settled. Cassie and Will have both found new beginnings in Wiscasset. And starting tonight, Martha Bailey"—she looked at Nathan with a smile—"no—Martha *Ames* will be here to help me. I think Martha and I can manage taking care of three men."

"And me, Ma," said Ethan. "Don't forget me!"

"We could never forget you, Ethan," said Ma, lifting him up and giving him a big hug. "How could we ever forget you?"

While the rest were putting Ma's contributions to the wedding feast into the wagon, Will walked up the hill to the small family cemetery. Here his great-grandparents and grandparents and aunts and uncles had been buried. Here he had played hide-and-seek behind the granite markers when he was Ethan's age, and here he had come when he needed to be alone.

He looked at the only new grave in the cemetery: the space where Pa had buried his leg. The toes that he had loved to wiggle in the mud, the shin he had bruised playing ball, and the knee he had banged coasting down the hill behind the schoolhouse on hand-hewn clapboards. "A part of me will always be here, on this farm," Will said softly to the grave. "It will stay here, even if I go away. I will miss the farm. I will miss Ma and Pa and my brothers. But it is time for me to go on."

He backed up a little, embarrassed to have caught himself talking out loud.

There on the ground next to him a black feather stood straight up in the soft, dark earth.

Down in the farmyard everyone was rushing about, readying gifts and food for the wedding. Nathan's life was changing today too. He would soon have a wife to love and protect and support. He did not have to leave home to move on.

"But I do," Will said to himself. This winter would be a test. If he failed, then he would try again. But he had to try. And he would need all the luck he could get. He thought of the old expression for surviving the freezing cold and dark days of a Maine winter.

"Winter well," Will whispered, looking out at the farm and family he loved. "And I pray that Cassie and I, too, will winter well."

He tucked the black feather in his pocket and continued down the hill.

HISTORICAL NOTES

The seaport of Wiscasset, Maine, shire town of Lincoln County since 1794, is on the Sheepscot River, about fifty miles northeast of Portland. During the late eighteenth and early nineteenth centuries it was one of the busiest ports east of Boston.

In 1819 and 1820 the area was recovering from the economic depression begun by the Embargo Act of 1807, continued by the War of 1812, and then made worse by several years of cold and drought that encouraged westward migration.

The District of Maine had been a part of Massachusetts Bay since 1652, when the Massachusetts General Court claimed it. During the Revolutionary War agitation for its own independence began in Maine, and finally, in 1819, a majority of Mainers voted for separation from Massachusetts. Under the Missouri Compromise of 1820, Maine entered the Union as a free state, Missouri was admitted as a slave state, and slavery was forbidden

in the Louisiana Territory north of the southern bound-
ary of Missouri. Today Maine honors its early association
with Massachusetts by being the only state other than
Massachusetts to celebrate Patriots' Day, commemorating
the battles of Lexington and Concord.

Compared with today's knowledge, the practice
of early-nineteenth-century medicine was primitive.
Although the concept of vaccination had been
tested, the connections between hygiene, germs, and
disease had not yet been made. Some surgical proce-
dures, such as amputation, were relatively common, but
their success was unpredictable even in the most sophis-
ticated European cities.

Until the middle of the nineteenth century there
was little formal training available for doctors. Some
American doctors were schooled in Europe like Dr.
Theobold's father, who attended medical lectures at a
German university and served as a doctor during the
American Revolution.

In 1820 formal medical training in the United
States consisted of a degree from one of the three arts
colleges (they became Harvard, Columbia, and the
University of Pennsylvania) that included lectures in
medicine, followed by an informal apprenticeship.
Many practicing doctors, like Dr. Theobold, had no
formal medical training and depended on experience
and medical journals for their knowledge.

Doctors of this period, especially those on the

frontier, often also served as dentists, surgeons, apothecaries, and even coffin makers.

By definition, doctors and surgeons were male.
Although some Native-American women were healers,
and women practicing as midwives performed vital services for women during the seventeenth and eighteenth
centuries, by 1820 male doctors in most towns and
cities of New England had convinced women that doctors were best qualified to assist during childbirth.
Midwives continued to serve women in frontier com-
munities throughout the nineteenth century, and during
the second half of the twentieth century there was a
resurgence of interest in the now medically certified
skill of midwifery.

Elizabeth Blackwell was the first American woman
to receive a medical degree in 1849. She, her sister (who
was also a doctor), and a female friend founded the
New York Infirmary for Women and Children in 1857.
Dr. Blackwell later settled in London, where she helped
establish the London School of Medicine for Women.

And although throughout history there have been
men and women who cared for the sick, there was no
formal training for nurses, male or female, in the United
States until 1873.

Thanksgiving, a harvest event first celebrated by the
Pilgrims in 1821, was observed in early December by
most eighteenth-century New Englanders. By 1819
there was little uniformity about the precise day on

which Thanksgiving was celebrated, but many states, even those outside New England, proclaimed it each year in November, and it had become a celebration of home-coming as well as of the harvest. In 1863 Abraham Lincoln made the third Thursday in November a national Thanksgiving Day, and in 1941 Congress passed a joint resolution moving it to the fourth Thursday in November.

The Ames family is fictional, as are Will's friends Sam and Paul, and the Pendleton brothers, but the other characters in *Wintering Well,* including Dr. Theobold and his family, lived and worked in Wiscasset, Maine, in 1819 and 1820. Dr. Theobold was a well-loved town doctor who was remembered for his caring, for his dogs, and for the roses that surrounded his Wiscasset home. After his wife, Nancy's, death in 1820 he remarried and continued to serve the people of Wiscasset until his death in 1846. His son, Fred, followed the family tra-dition and also became a doctor.

The Wiscasset jail that Will and Dr. Theobold visi-ted was used until 1953. Today it, and the jailer's home, are cared for by the Lincoln County Historical Society and are open to the public during summer months.

And an old letter in the Wiscasset archives tells the story of a boy who fooled the other boys in town by moving a flock of sheep into the graveyard and pre-tending to be afraid of the ghosts there.